Medicine

Other books in the Careers for the Twenty-First Century series:

Aeronautics
Law Enforcement
The News Media

Careers
for the
Twenty-First
Century

Medicine

by Beverly Britton

LUCENT BOOKS
SAN DIEGO, CALIFORNIA

THOMSON

GALE

Detroit • New York • San Diego • San Francisco
Boston • New Haven, Conn. • Waterville, Maine
London • Munich

Library of Congress Cataloging-in-Publication Data

Britton, Beverly.
  Medicine / by Beverly Britton.
    p. cm. — (Careers for the 21st century)
Includes bibliographical references and index.
Summary: Describes the job outlook and required training, education, and
qualifications for the healthcare career positions of nurse, physician, medical
technologist, physical therapist, pharmacist, and emergency medical technician.
    ISBN 1-56006-888-4
    1. Medicine—Vocational guidance—Juvenile literature. [1. Medicine—
Vocational guidance. 2. Vocational guidance.] I. Title. II. Careers for the
21st century (San Diego, Calif.)
  R690 .B675 2002
  610.69—dc21

2001003019

Contents

Foreword

Young people in the twenty-first century are faced with a dizzying array of possibilities for careers as they become adults. However, the advances of technology and a world economy in which events in one nation increasingly affect events in other nations have made the job market extremely competitive. Young people entering the job market today must possess a combination of technological knowledge and an understanding of the cultural and socioeconomic factors that affect the working world. Don Tapscott, internationally known author and consultant on the effects of technology in business, government, and society, supports this idea, saying, "Yes, this country needs more technology graduates, as they fuel the digital economy. But . . . we have an equally strong need for those with a broader [humanities] background who can work in tandem with technical specialists, helping create and manage the [workplace] environment." To succeed in this job market young people today must enter it with a certain amount of specialized knowledge, preparation, and practical experience. In addition, they must possess the drive to update their job skills continually to match rapidly occurring technological, economic, and social changes.

Young people entering the twenty-first-century job market must carefully research and plan the education and training they will need to work in their chosen career. High school graduates can no longer go straight into a job where they can hope to advance to positions of higher pay, better working conditions, and increased responsibility without first entering a training program, trade school, or college. For example, aircraft mechanics must attend schools that offer Federal Aviation Administration–accredited programs. These programs offer a broad-based curriculum that requires students to demonstrate an understanding of the basic principles of flight, aircraft function, and electronics. Students must also master computer technology used for diagnosing problems and show that they can apply what they learn toward routine maintenance and any number of needed repairs. With further education, an aircraft mechanic can gain increasingly specialized licenses that place him or her in the job market for positions of higher pay and greater responsibility.

In addition to technology skills, young people must understand how to communicate and work effectively with colleagues or clients from diverse backgrounds. James Billington, librarian of Congress, ascertains that "we do not have a global village, but rather a globe on which there are a whole lot of new villages . . . each trying to get its own place in the world, and anybody who's going to deal with this world is going to have to relate better to more of it." For example, flight attendants are increasingly being expected to know one or more foreign languages in order for them to better serve the needs of international passengers. Electrical engineers collaborating with a sister company in Russia on a project must be aware of cultural differences that could affect communication between the project members and, ultimately, the success of the project.

The Lucent Books Careers for the Twenty-First Century series discusses how these ideas come into play in such competitive career fields as aeronautics, biotechnology, computer technology, engineering, education, law enforcement, and medicine. Each title in the series discusses from five to seven different careers available in the respective field. The series provides a comprehensive view of what it's like to work in a particular job and what it takes to succeed in it. Each chapter encompasses a career's most recent trends in education and training, job responsibilities, the work environment and conditions, special challenges, earnings, and opportunities for advancement. Primary and secondary source quotes enliven the text. Sidebars expand on issues related to each career, including topics such as gender issues in the workplace, personal stories that demonstrate exceptional on the job experiences, and the latest technology and its potential for use in a particular career. Every volume includes an Organizations to Contact list as well as annotated bibliographies. Books in this series provide readers with pertinent information for deciding on a career, and a launching point for further research.

Combining Science and Service

The field of medicine attracts those who are interested in being of service to others and who have an interest in science. The field is unique because it combines the use of technology with close human contact. Those who work in the health care field use everything from computers to ventilators, all requiring an understanding of scientific principles. That scientific knowledge is then used to work closely with individuals with health problems.

Medical professions require a background in science before entering the field. It is essential for anyone entering a health care career to have an interest in science. In choosing a career, Tim Thornton, a pharmacist, says, "I just looked at my strengths in high school and saw my biggest strengths were math and science."[1] This was a deciding factor in his decision to enter pharmacy. High school courses in such subjects as anatomy, biology, chemistry, and physics were helpful preparation.

In addition to knowledge in science, a quality shared by many who choose a career in medicine is the desire to help people. Health care workers, for the most part, work very closely with patients. Nurses, physicians, physical therapists, and emergency medical technicians spend the majority of their day in direct contact with people who are acutely ill, are in emergency situations, or are being rehabilitated following an illness or injury. For example, the opportunity to be of service and to make a difference appeals to many who choose nursing as a career. Mary Mallison, a former editor of the

American Journal of Nursing, explains the unique relationship between nurses and patients: "A lot of nursing resembles the best kind of parenting. Supporting people until they can help themselves and strengthening their belief in themselves."[2]

Pharmacists and medical technologists have less direct patient contact than other health care workers, but they still work with patients by educating them about medications or, in the case of technologists, by drawing blood samples when other lab personnel are not available to do it. There is a lot of satisfaction in being able to help people. Kenneth Callen, a physician in the state of Washington, says, "Probably the most important advantage comes from helping people who are sick."[3]

Jobs in health care require highly skilled workers. It is not possible to obtain any of these positions without specialized training and usually a college education. Preparation for a medical career can begin in high school with health occupations classes, in which students observe or participate in activities in hospitals, physicians'

A nursing student prepares an IV in a university classroom.

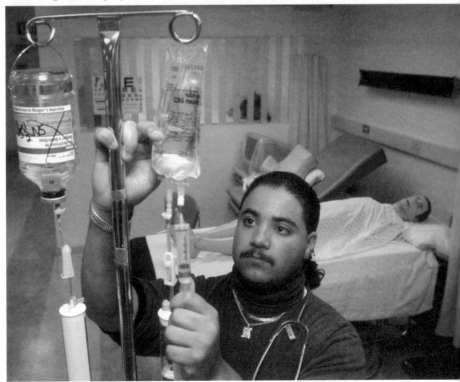

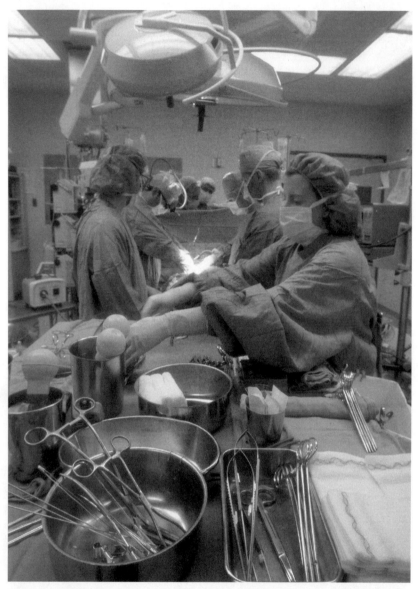

The U.S. health care system employs over 11 million people nationwide.

offices, and outpatient health care agencies such as kidney dialysis centers. Gary Bennett describes an opportunity for students and others to get firsthand experience by observing his job as an emergency medical technician (EMT). "If you are considering it [a career as an EMT], a lot of services will let you do what they call 'ride-alongs' and you get to go and get to be an observer to actual calls." He says, "We do that quite often."[4]

Health occupations classes in high school can be a helpful way to explore health careers. Kelly Bartek, a physical therapist at the Texas Sports Medicine Center, says that she made her decision to become a therapist while in a high school health occupations class. By attending the classes and by visiting hospitals, she says, "I was able to be exposed to physical therapy and that helped me make the decision. It seemed like every therapist I talked to loved their job."[5]

Although college prepares one for a career in the field, medical knowledge changes rapidly. Most professional careers in health care mandate continuing education so practitioners stay current. A career in medicine carries the tremendous responsibility of managing the health and well-being of patients. Mistakes can have disastrous consequences, so workers need to perform their jobs at the highest level possible by keeping their knowledge base up-to-date.

The U.S. health care industry is one of the largest employers in the country with over 11 million jobs, making it a field in which employment opportunities abound. Out of thirty jobs predicted by the government to grow the fastest in the beginning of the twenty-first century, twelve are in health care.

Registered nurses, who occupy about 2 million jobs, are the largest professional group in the health care field. Physicians rank second in number with 586,000 jobs. In descending order of number of workers are medical technology, physical therapy, pharmacy, and emergency medical services. The Bureau of Labor Statistics predicts a percentage increase in jobs in these six categories from 11 to 37 percent by 2008, depending on the profession. Emergency medical technicians top the list with a 37 percent increase.

Job opportunities in health care fields are continually increasing, with population changes in the United States contributing to this growth. A growing and aging population increases the need for health care workers. With the U.S. population expected to increase another 23 million by the year 2008, more workers in all health care fields are needed to care for the sick. Jobs in medicine will be plentiful and will offer exciting, challenging work for those interested in serving others in a science-related profession.

Chapter 1

Nurses

Nurses provide health care to people with illnesses and also to those who want to maintain their health. Nurses are the health care professionals who spend the most time with individual patients. In a hospital setting, nurses work with an assigned group of patients for eight to twelve hours a day. This is in contrast to physicians, who see patients once or twice a day for only a few minutes, or physical therapists, who spend from ten to sixty minutes providing services for a single patient before moving on to other patients.

The duties of nurses have greatly expanded in the past thirty years. Previously, nurses administered medications, made beds, accompanied physicians on hospital rounds to visit patients, and were responsible for ensuring that doctors' orders for tests and treatments were carried out. Although some of these same tasks are still part of a nurse's job, nurses today perform more than basic bedside comfort measures. "A lot of people see nursing as bedpans and sponge baths, but that isn't the case anymore,"[6] says Jen Macri, who is an intensive care nurse in Oak Lawn, Illinois. Nurses today work with ventilators, which help patients breathe, know how to read electrocardiographs (tracings of the heart's rhythm), and administer high-powered drugs into surgically implanted lines running directly into major blood vessels.

The career of nursing has progressed into a high-tech field while still maintaining its personal relationship with patients. Rosemary Luquire, a vice president for patient care at St. Luke's Episcopal Hospital in Houston, says, "Nurses today must be so well-educated that they can routinely use multimillion dollar space-age equipment while still delivering the emotional support that means so much to a patient's recovery."[7]

The Duties of a Registered Nurse

Because nurses spend the most time with hospitalized patients, their hours on duty are filled with tasks designed to help the patient get well as quickly as possible. There are two types of nurses that perform these tasks: registered nurses (RNs) and licensed practical nurses (LPNs).

Registered nurses are responsible for seeing that physicians' written orders for patients are carried out. They also are independently responsible for planning nursing care for assigned patients and for ensuring that it is completed. This could include everything from patient education to setting up schedules for turning bedridden patients. Since licensed practical nurses and nurses' aides perform some of this planned work, part of a registered nurse's job is supervising their work.

A registered nurse works closely with the physician and patient.

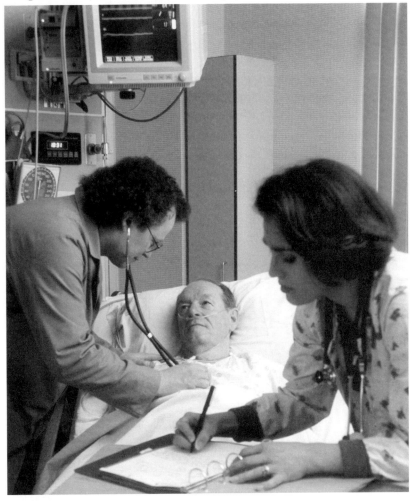

During a typical shift, RNs administer medications, including intravenous medications (IVs) and injections. They must watch for signs and symptoms of complications and report them to physicians. Sandy Cacciatore, a registered nurse in a Houston suburb, says that during her first year as a nurse she was "overwhelmed with the idea that someone's health was in my hands. I didn't want to miss signs that the patient was developing a complication."[8] Nurses check results from patients' laboratory tests, recognize normal versus abnormal results, and use this information to safely administer medications and keep the physician informed about possible problems.

The responsibility of being in charge of a patient for many hours each day means a nurse must recognize slight changes in a patient's condition. Nurses do this by performing a physical assessment on each patient at the beginning of every shift. The nurse checks the patient's temperature, pulse, respirations, and blood pressure and listens to lung, heart, and bowel sounds with a stethoscope. Another duty is checking lines and tubes for proper functioning and dressings for drainage. Nurses also question patients about their current symptoms.

Nurses provide information about the patient's care to the patient and to the patient's family members. This can include facts about drugs being administered, the purpose of tests being performed, or anything the patient or family will need to know once the patient leaves the hospital.

Communication with physicians and other health care workers is a necessary part of a nurse's job. It is important to keep other medical personnel informed of the current status of the patient since numerous people care for each patient during a hospitalization. This communication takes many forms, including documentation on each patient's chart, end-of-shift reports to the oncoming nurses, and conversations with the patient's physician by phone or in person.

The Duties of a Licensed Practical Nurse

Another type of nurse who has a lot of patient contact is a licensed practical nurse. Licensed practical nurses or licensed vocational nurses (LVNs) are two titles given to the same job. The states of California and Texas are the only two states calling these nurses LVNs. Licensed practical nurses provide basic bedside care, which may involve many of the same duties as registered nurses, including administering medications, assessing patients for changes in condition, and documenting care on the patient's chart.

Nursing Licensure

In order to use the titles *registered nurse (RN)* or *licensed practical* or *vocational nurse (LPN or LVN)*, graduates of nursing schools need to pass a national licensing exam. These exams are referred to as state boards because they are administered by the state where graduation occurred. Registered nurses and licensed practical nurses have separate exams. The registered nurse exam is called the National Council Licensure Examination-RN, and the practical nurse exam is called the National Council Licensure Examination-PN.

To be eligible to take the examination, a student must have graduated from a state accredited nursing program. In addition, most states will ask applicants some personal history questions related to mental illness, substance abuse, and criminal offenses. The purpose of these questions is to prevent issuing a license to nurses who might not be emotionally or ethically fit to care for patients.

The applicant takes the examination by computer at a state-approved testing site. It covers nursing care for a variety of diseases, knowledge of nutrition and pharmacology, communication skills, and issues related to patient safety. The examination can last from one to five hours, depending on how well students do on a series of progressively more difficult questions. There are fees for both taking the examination and for getting a license.

Once a license is obtained, it must be renewed periodically— typically every two years. Some states require nurses to obtain a certain number of hours of continuing education in order to be allowed to renew their licenses.

Although the duties are similar, LPNs work under the supervision of RNs because they have less formal nursing education. Licensed practical nurses have more limited supervisory duties than RNs, usually only having responsibility for supervising other LPNs or nurses' aides. Although the director of a nursing home may be an RN, LPNs who work in nursing homes are frequently in charge of whole units of patients and the staff who care for them because, unlike hospitals, these facilities do not care for acutely ill patients.

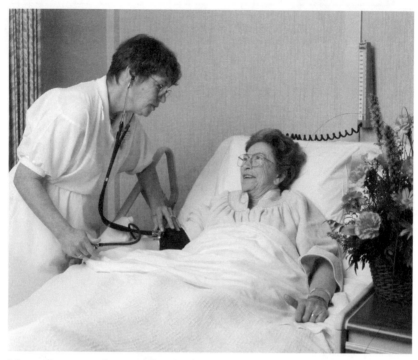

Hospital nurses often spend eight or more hours on their feet.

Personal Qualifications

Nurses need a variety of characteristics to be good at their profession. Pediatric nurse practitioner (a registered nurse with additional training in pediatrics and usually a master's degree) Catherine Ernsthausen says, "I think there are many qualities a nurse should have, including problem-solving skills, patience, and energy."[9] Because a nurse works with people from all walks of life and all age groups, the ability to communicate by speaking clearly and listening carefully is important. Nurses deal with patients who often are in crisis due to their illnesses, so they must have patience, understanding, and the ability to maintain a calm, professional manner at all times. For example, patients who are just beginning to deal with a new diagnosis of a serious illness are not always grateful for the care they receive and can even seem rude because their emotional energy is needed to cope with their illness. Nurses need good mental health to be compassionate in this situation.

A nurse must have the ability to set priorities because nurses frequently face many tasks at once. Nurses have to decide which jobs require immediate attention and which can wait a few minutes. It is not unusual for two or three patients to ask for help at the same time. For instance, one patient might ask for a glass of water, one might want pain medication, and another help turning in bed. In this situation the need for pain medication would be the priority. Good organizational skills and the ability to follow instructions are helpful when juggling multiple tasks.

Taking care of patients all day is tiring, so nurses must have good physical health. Most nursing jobs require a lot of energy and opportunities to sit are limited. Hospital nurses frequently spend eight or more hours per shift on their feet, walking between patient rooms and helping to lift or turn patients, so back injuries can be an occupational hazard.

Many nurses find that the variety the job offers and the feeling of accomplishment are two of the most appealing aspects. Cacciatore says,

> One of the things I love about nursing is meeting so many kinds of people—not only cultural differences, but personality differences, and lifestyle differences. It is constantly intriguing—it never gets boring. No two days are the same . . . but what I really like best is knowing that when I go to work, the job I do is a really important job. Someone is really counting on me. It is going to make a difference in someone's life. I like that.[10]

Because nurses spend more time with patients than any other health care professional, enjoying close personal contact with people is essential. Cacciatore has definite ideas about what the main qualification for nursing is:

> Don't rule it out because you don't like blood or because you're nervous about shots. You get over that part fairly quickly. The thing to think about when you are looking at your career is do you love people? Do you like to help people, or would you like to sit at a desk and not deal with people too much? A nurse needs to be someone who truly enjoys people. I think that is the main criteria.[11]

Three Educational Paths for RNs

Nursing is unique because there are three educational paths that can qualify a person to take the national licensure examination to become a registered nurse. These are associate degree programs, diploma programs, and baccalaureate (four-year) degree programs. Associate degree nursing programs are two-year programs usually offered in community or junior colleges. They combine basic academic courses such as English, history, and science with specific nursing courses covering disease processes and recommended care. Actual experience with patient care complements the academic work.

Diploma schools of nursing are three-year programs managed by hospitals. They are the oldest of the three programs, and at one time most registered nurses were graduates of diploma schools. In the last thirty-five years the number of these schools has decreased because, during the 1960s, the American Nurses' Association stated a preference for university programs that led to a four-year degree in nursing. This route was considered to produce nurses with a more well-rounded education, and it was thought a bachelor's degree was more in line with education of other health care professions. Despite this, graduation from diploma programs still qualifies a student to take the national examination to become an RN. Diploma programs include basic academic courses plus nursing courses, but their strength is their emphasis on patient care. Diploma graduates typically spend more time in hospitals and clinics doing patient care than graduates of other nursing programs.

Bachelor degree programs are available through four-year colleges and universities, and graduates of these programs receive a bachelor of science degree in nursing. A few of the programs are five years in length. Typically, the first two years consist of prerequisite courses like English, history, government, psychology, and science courses. The last two or three years are spent taking specific nursing courses teaching the care of pediatric, obstetric, psychiatric, medical, and surgical patients. Students spend about two days a week in a hospital or other health care setting actually caring for patients.

All nursing programs offer a variety of patient care experiences during the educational process. A student on a surgical unit is assigned two to three patients to care for and monitors their progress after surgery, administers medications, writes notes on the patients' charts, and bathes the patients. As the student gains experience, more complex patient care is assigned. In addition to assignments on the usual patient care units, specialty units such as renal dialysis, intensive care, and emergency rooms are included. Most programs

Men in Nursing

Nursing has been predominantly a female profession since the early 1900s. In recent years the number of men entering nursing has increased. Today, slightly more than 5 percent of all nurses in the United States are men, an increase from 1 percent in 1966. Many men are drawn to nursing after serving as medics in the military or after a career as an emergency medical technician. An improvement in salaries is also a factor in making the profession more attractive to men.

The idea of men working as nurses is not new. History indicates that a nursing school for men existed in 350 B.C. in India. There are records of men as nurses during the Middle Ages, during ancient plagues, and during the Civil War. However, from 1900 to the late 1950s, women dominated the field of nursing. Men were denied admission to female nursing schools and were not allowed to serve as nurses in the military even if they were trained as a nurse by one of the few all-male nursing schools. In fact, it was a female nursing organization established during the early 1900s that was responsible for barring males from serving as nurses in the military. After the Korean War of the 1950s, men regained military nursing positions and gradually were allowed admission to nursing schools that were formerly all female.

As the number of men in nursing increased, the need for an organization to support them became evident. The American Assembly for Men in Nursing (AAMN) is an organization designed to discuss issues that affect men in the nursing profession. Issues addressed by the AAMN include male health problems, the need to encourage men of all ages to enter nursing, and the support of men in nursing to grow professionally. This group has a website (aamn.freeyellow.com) and holds an annual convention.

also offer experience in outpatient settings like home health or hospice, the care of the dying.

The classes offered in nursing school are unlike other college classes. Students are expected to problem solve when caring for patients by taking information from class and applying it to actual situations. For example, a student caring for a diabetic patient would be expected to recognize the differences between a patient with high versus low blood sugar and should know the correct action to take in each case. Cacciatore, who graduated from an associate degree program, comments on her experience in nursing school: "Nursing school was different [from prerequisite courses like English or microbiology] in that you had to learn facts and then apply them to situations."[12] Cacciatore admits that nursing school was hard, but "I loved learning about the body and diseases and how they affected us."[13]

Regardless from which type of program a person graduates, the designation registered nurse (RN) cannot be used until a person passes a national licensure examination typically given within two weeks to two months after graduation from a state accredited nursing school. State laws require this license in order to be employed as a nurse.

Nursing students practice in a classroom prior to receiving their nursing license.

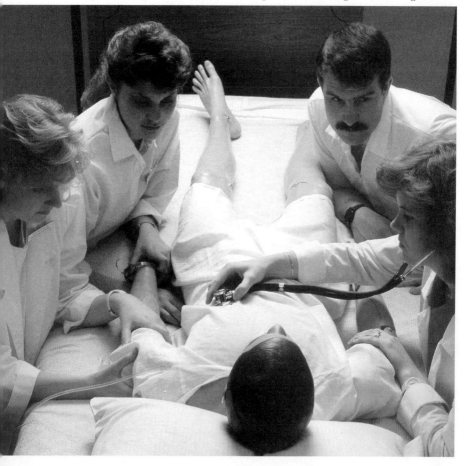

Becoming a Nurse in One Year

The training of a licensed practical nurse takes place over a shorter period of time than is required for a registered nurse. LPNs are educated for one full year in a program administered by a hospital, a board of education, or a community college or vocational school. A few programs take eighteen months. The typical program requires a high school diploma or a high school equivalency certificate for admission, but not college prerequisites as the RN programs do. The program is time intensive; classes and patient care experience may require thirty-five to forty hours a week at school.

Students in these programs receive instruction in all required subjects and obtain clinical experience within one year. They study shorter courses of the basic sciences, like anatomy, physiology, nutrition, and microbiology, which RN students must take before entry into their programs. Like registered nurses, practical nurses must take a national licensure examination.

Job Opportunities

Nursing is a career that offers a variety of settings in which to work. However, new graduates of nursing programs, either RN or LPN, are usually encouraged to work for one year as a staff nurse, an entry-level position, on a medical-surgical hospital unit before attempting to specialize. This gives them a broad, experience-based background, which is helpful in areas such as intensive care, pediatrics, obstetrics, home health, surgery, or emergency rooms.

The variety of work settings available is a positive aspect of nursing. There are as many different jobs in nursing as there are personalities. For those who like excitement, the emergency room is an area of interest. People who are good communicators usually find psychiatric nursing a rewarding area. Nurses who enjoy working with high-tech equipment often like intensive care. Those who prefer working with children will find opportunities in a newborn nursery or in pediatrics.

Licensed practical nurses have some of the same opportunities but may be denied certain positions because of their lack of a degree. The *Occupational Outlook Handbook*, a government publication that describes jobs and predicts their growth, states that nursing homes over the next eight years will offer the most new jobs for LPNs, but LPNs who seek jobs in hospitals may face competition from RNs.

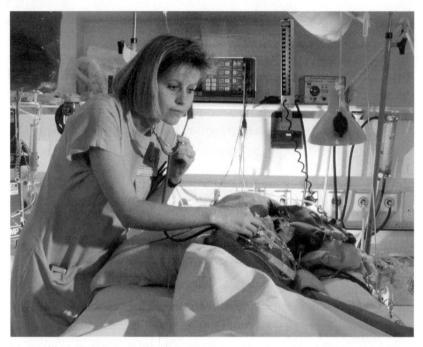

Registered nurses are the largest professional group in the health care field.

According to this same source, in 1998, 32 percent of LPNs worked in hospitals, 28 percent worked in nursing homes, and 14 percent in doctors' offices or clinics.

Employment as a nurse is one of the most secure jobs there is. The *Occupational Outlook Handbook* says that nursing is the largest health care occupation, employing more people than any other health care profession. Registered nurses held about 2.1 million jobs in 1998. Over 80 percent of registered nurses in the United States are employed. Despite this, there are more nursing jobs than there are nurses available to fill them.

Although three out of five RNs work in hospitals, nursing offers many other positions and settings in which to practice, including home health, outpatient surgical and birthing centers, and extended-care homes. The government offers nursing opportunities in the military, in Veterans Administration hospitals, and in Indian Health Services. Large medical centers and some physicians' offices conduct research and employ nurses, usually those with advanced education, to assist with gathering information. Nurses also work as consultants in law firms and for health insurance companies and as manufacturers' representatives for medical products.

Sandy Cacciatore's experience illustrates the variety of employment opportunities available in the field of nursing. Her first job was in a pediatrician's office. She eventually left there to work in a hospital as a staff nurse on a medical-surgical unit. "I always had in mind to be a hospital nurse,"[14] says Cacciatore. The floor where she worked took care of patients before and after surgery, but it also treated patients with a wide variety of diseases. After three years at this job, Cacciatore was offered an opportunity to combine the hospital job with a job as a lab instructor for student nurses from the same college she had attended. Under this arrangement, she worked as a hospital nurse part of the week and spent the remainder of the week working with student nurses as they learned nursing skills in a laboratory setting.

Flexible Schedules

Anyone considering nursing as a career should be aware that hospital positions, as well as some other nursing jobs, require working some weekends and holidays. New graduates sometimes have difficulty finding day shift positions and may instead have to work evening or night shifts. The ability to work nights or evenings appeals to people whose responsibilities at home or personal habits make daytime work schedules unattractive. Cacciatore's work schedule is also an example of the variety available for nurses. She has worked full time with eight-hour shifts and has also worked part time when she combined hospital nursing with her job working with student nurses. Her work schedule has included both the day and evening shifts.

A nursing career offers flexibility in the number of hours a nurse wants to work. Typical hospital shifts run from 7:00 A.M. to 3:00 P.M., 3:00 to 11:00 P.M., or 11:00 P.M. to 7:00 A.M. A nurse may work eight-hour shifts five days a week or twelve-hour shifts three days a week. Nurses who prefer a regular Monday through Friday work schedule may seek employment in school clinics or in physicians' offices. The opportunity to work part time is appealing to many nurses who want to have more time at home with their children. There are many opportunities for part-time work as evidenced by the *Occupational Outlook Handbook*'s statement that one out of four RNs works part time.

Moving Up

The two best ways to earn a promotion in nursing are through experience over time or by obtaining additional education. The

Occupational Outlook Handbook says that graduates of baccalaureate programs have greater advancement opportunities than graduates of diploma or associate degree RN programs or graduates of LPN programs. Approximately 40 percent of LPNs use their practical nursing license as a stepping-stone to other health occupations. Many head nurses have achieved their positions simply by good job performance. Most management-level positions, such as a nurse manager or a vice president or president of a nursing care facility, require a master's degree or doctorate in nursing or business management in addition to a bachelor's degree in nursing.

None of the programs for RNs or LPNs prepares a nurse for a specialty care position such as operating room nurse, labor and delivery nurse, intensive care nurse, or emergency room nurse. Although students receive some experience in these areas during nursing school, it does not qualify them to work in these positions once they graduate. Specialization can be achieved with on-the-job training or with advanced nursing degrees.

Some nurses want to specialize, and this can require experience, additional training, or both. For example, nurse-anesthetists, who administer anesthesia under a doctor's supervision, must attend additional schooling to qualify. Some programs require prior experience as an intensive care nurse, and most require two to three years of education beyond a bachelor's degree to qualify to administer anesthesia. National certification is required to become a certified registered nurse-anesthetist. Bertha Lovelace, a nurse-anesthetist in Cleveland, Ohio, explains her job: "Basically, a nurse-anesthetist is responsible for keeping the patient anesthetized and free of pain during an operation. She or he is also responsible for bringing the patient back to a state of wakefulness afterward."[15]

For some nurses, nothing is more rewarding than providing care to expectant mothers and delivering their babies. Those who want to enter this field can, after basic nursing school, attend a midwifery school, take a certification exam, and become certified nurse-midwives. "Bringing babies into this world is a calling. My three years at North Central Bronx Hospital allowed me the privilege of witnessing dozens of miracles a week,"[16] says Jane Arnold, a nurse-midwife. This nursing role is different from that of a lay midwife, who does not have to be a nurse and whose only training is an apprenticeship with another midwife.

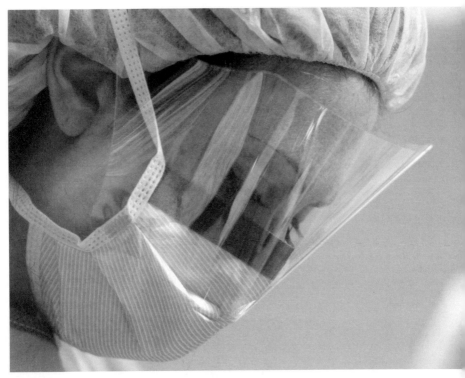

A nurse assists during cardiac surgery.

A position that attracts a lot of nurses is that of nurse-practitioner. These nurses usually have master's degrees along with education that allows them to examine and diagnose patients and write prescriptions. They usually work in an office with a physician and see patients by appointment in much the same way physicians do. Most nurse-practitioners have a specialty, such as adult health, family health, or pediatrics. Brad Potts, a nurse-practitioner in family practice, says, "My patients are anywhere from two weeks old to elderly. Initially, we do a head-to-toe physical and a complete health assessment. If it's a common health problem, we can handle it ourselves [meaning without a physician's help]."[17]

Another field that nurses work in is law. Some nurses use their nursing education, combined with a law degree, to practice medical malpractice defense or prosecution. Those who do not want to attend law school may find positions as legal nurse consultants. These nurses work for law firms and provide expert advice on cases concerning health care issues. Nurses who do this usually have years of experience in a specialty area or have an advanced degree.

Salaries for Nurses

Salaries for nurses have improved over the last thirty years. According to a survey published in April 2000, conducted by the journal *Nursing 2000*, the mean starting rate for new RNs is $15.41 per hour; for a new LPN, $11.65 per hour. This same survey showed RNs with less than five years' experience earning $41,393 a year. Salaries are highest in states bordering the Pacific Ocean, where the cost of living is higher, and lowest in states along the lower Atlantic such as Florida, Georgia, the Virginias, and the Carolinas. The *Nursing 2000* survey also revealed that hospital nurses earn the most, with home health care nurses a close second. Of nurses who earn a master of science degree in nursing, 40 percent earn more than $50,000 a year.

In addition to regular salaries, most hospitals pay higher hourly wages for evening or night shifts than for day shifts. Another method

The Nursing Shortage

The twenty-first century offers numerous opportunities for a career in nursing. An acute nursing shortage is predicted to last several years. The *Occupational Outlook Handbook* for 1998 through 2008, which is published by the government and predicts employment trends in many job fields, says the number of available jobs in nursing is second only to the number of job openings for computer systems analysts. Several states, such as Massachusetts, New York, California, and Texas, have issued reports about the current shortage. A report from Texas states that even in 1998, approximately forty thousand more registered nurses were needed in Texas alone.

The nursing shortage is due to several factors. Fewer people chose nursing careers during the last part of the twentieth century because more occupations were available to women, who make up the largest number of nurses. A second reason for the shortage is a trend of early retirement for nurses. Currently only 9 percent of nurses are under the age of thirty. This means there is a continuing need as older nurses, who make up the greatest percentage of nurses, retire. A final reason is that the population in the United States is growing older, and older people require more medical care.

hospital nurses use to increase their earnings is to work additional shifts.

Nurses who decide to continue their education and work in a specialty area receive higher salaries than nurses with only a basic nursing education. The median annual salary for a certified nurse-anesthetist is $84,000, according to a survey by the American Association of Nurse Anesthetists. Certified nurse-midwives average between $54,600 and $68,500 a year, and full-time nurse-practitioners earned $61,488 on average in the year 2000. Salaries for nurse-practitioners, however, can vary depending on the specialty area. Nurses who work in medical legal consulting work mostly part time to supplement incomes from their regular nursing jobs and are paid between $75 and $150 an hour.

Nursing in the Twenty-First Century

Nursing is a career with excellent opportunities for the future. Employment has been good for many years and will continue to be good into the twenty-first century. The Bureau of Labor Statistics lists registered nursing as one of the ten occupations with the largest job growth for 1998–2008. The number of jobs available is greater than almost any other profession, either in or out of the health care field. Compared to other health care positions, nurses have one of the widest ranges of work settings, making nursing a career that can appeal to all types of people. For anyone who enjoys working closely with people, nursing is a good career for the twenty-first century.

Chapter 2

Physicians

Physicians are the leaders of the health care team, which means the physician is ultimately responsible for the patient's well-being. After determining the cause of a patient's illness, physicians prescribe a treatment plan and write orders for care, which frequently are carried out by other health care workers. The physician's orders guide the work of nurses, pharmacists, medical technologists, physical therapists, and all others caring for a patient. As a result of this great responsibility, physicians, on average, earn almost twice as much per year as the next highest paid health care professional. Having the responsibility for managing a patient's illness also means that physicians work long hours since they are caring for patients seen both in the office and those who are hospitalized.

Examining, Diagnosing, and Treating

Two types of physicians provide health care leadership. The 586,000 medical doctors (MDs) in the United States are the larger group. Osteopathic physicians (DOs—doctors of osteopathic medicine) are fewer in number, with 38,000 physicians, but their number is growing. The role of either type of physician involves diagnosing illnesses and prescribing treatment for people who are injured or who have a disease. Medical and osteopathic physicians treat illnesses in much the same way, with one difference. Medical doctors rely on medications, surgery, radiation, and physical therapy to treat illnesses. Osteopathic physicians use these same four methods, but also perform manipulative therapy by using their hands to move muscles and bones into proper positions to restore health.

In order to diagnose an illness, all physicians begin by taking a medical history and by performing a physical exam. The history involves asking questions about the patient's current symptoms and past medical problems. Erin Cardon, a general internist in women's wellness in Connecticut, says, "It is only in being attentive to the

28

patient, truly listening and ultimately caring about what is said, that the art of diagnosis reveals itself."[18]

After the history is complete, the physician concentrates the examination on the affected part of the body. During this examination a physician may use a stethoscope to auscultate (listen) to the heart, lungs, or bowel sounds to detect problems. Physicians also use otoscopes to examine the inside of the ear or an ophthalmoscope to inspect the interior of the eye. Both instruments use light and magnification. When a physician presses on an area of the body to check for pain or abnormalities, this technique is known as palpation. Another method of examination is percussion, which involves thumping on parts of the body to listen for changes in sound, which might indicate an unseen growth or internal abnormality. The simplest method of examining a patient is inspection, during which the physician looks for changes in the skin and outer parts of the body.

On completion of the examination, the physician may order diagnostic tests to help determine the cause of the symptoms. These can include blood or urine test or X rays. Other more sophisticated tests, such as ultrasounds, which use reflected sound waves to study

A physician performs a basic check-up on a young patient.

internal body parts, and MRIs (magnetic resonance imaging), which scan the internal body to provide a detailed image, are sometimes needed to help with the diagnosis.

Once the history, physical, and diagnostic tests are complete, the physician reviews this information, makes a diagnosis, and prescribes a plan of care. The treatment plan may be simple enough for the patient to follow at home with no professional help or it may require the services of other health care workers.

Since there are approximately thirty-five specialties from which doctors can choose to practice, the duties of the physician can vary depending on the area of specialization. Some of the areas physicians

The American Medical Association

The American Medical Association (AMA) is the main professional organization for medical doctors. Nathan Smith Davis, a doctor from western New York, founded the American Medical Association over 150 years ago. Davis belonged to his state's medical society, but no national medical association existed. He proposed the establishment of a national association to elevate the standard of medical practice in the United States. Along with other doctors in favor of this idea, he helped form the AMA in 1847. Davis served as president of the association during the Civil War and was the first editor of the *Journal of the American Medical Association*, the organization's professional publication.

The AMA promotes the science and art of medicine and the betterment of public health. The AMA does this by speaking out on behalf of physicians and patients and by discussing national health issues such as the effects of smoking and adolescent health problems. The AMA develops national health recommendations in much the same way the government does its work. There is a house of delegates in which state, local, and physician-specialty groups send representatives to meetings that occur twice a year. The association sets policy using a democratic process and then works with government agencies to bring about recommended changes.

A physician's job includes communicating information to patients in an understandable way.

can specialize in include pediatrics, family practice, internal medicine, and psychiatry.

Personal Qualifications

Regardless of the type of physician, the ability to provide direction for a health care team and to accept the responsibility that accompanies that position are important characteristics. Physicians constantly make decisions that can affect individuals and their ability to live a healthy life. In an emergency, a doctor must remain calm while deciding on a course of action. When a patient experiences a medical crisis, a doctor must quickly determine the cause of the problem, decide on a plan of action, and then direct the members of the team to begin treatment. The constant stress of making important decisions concerning health matters requires an emotionally stable personality, able to withstand stress. Inability to work under stress can lead to poor decision-making on the part of the doctor.

Because of their roles as health care leaders, physicians must be intelligent. Caring for patients and directing the care of other health care workers requires a large body of knowledge. Physicians have to enjoy the challenge of learning and using complex scientific information. Mary Alfano, a family practice physician in Michigan, says, "It was the intellectual challenge that first attracted me to medicine."[19]

A physician should enjoy talking to patients, be a good listener, and be able to communicate information in an understandable way to resolve health problems. The ability to translate complex medical information into plain language requires both intelligence and a desire to help patients understand their illnesses. Erin Cardon explains how her decision to become a physician was influenced by two things she enjoyed: "I decided to go into medicine as a career because it combined my love of science and working with people."[20] The desire to work with people in a science-related profession is the central characteristic of a good physician.

Being a physician requires working long and irregular hours. Dan Hurwitz, a family practitioner, says, "A typical day starts with me getting up in the morning around 5:30, quarter to 6."[21] He says he does paperwork he has brought home from the hospital for thirty to forty-five minutes every morning. "Then I'll go to the hospital and make rounds. My first [office] appointment is at nine o'clock."[22] The *Occupational Outlook Handbook* says that more than one-third of all full-time physicians worked sixty hours or more a week in 1998. Physicians frequently take calls after office hours and on weekends and make emergency visits to hospitals.

From Premed Through Medical School

Not only does a career as a physician require intelligence and dedication, but it also requires a long period of education in order to practice medicine. Medical students spend eleven to fifteen years in school after high school. This includes four years of college (although a few medical schools will accept students after three years), four years of medical school, and three to seven years in a residency program where additional information is gained in a specialty area. The number of years of education is related to the type of medicine the physician wishes to practice.

To prepare for medical school, students are required to take physics, biology, mathematics, English, and chemistry during the first four years of college. English is important because the entrance exam for acceptance into medical school scores students on writing skills as one of its criteria and because communication with patients and other health care workers is such an important part of the job. Social sciences, such as psychology courses, are important for future patient contact and for developing an awareness of the psychological aspects of illness. Most four-year colleges have a premed curriculum that includes these courses.

During the four years of premed courses, many students choose to major in one of the life sciences, such as chemistry or biology, although other college majors are allowed as long as the required courses are completed. Good grades are important since students entering medical school in the year 2000 had a grade point average of 3.6 (B+). Only one out of three applicants is accepted into medical school, so students interested in this career should strive to maintain a good grade point average. Hurwitz offers this advice: "Getting into medical school is exceedingly difficult. Probably the most important thing for a student considering a premed course is that the first year in college is most important. If you start out with a low GPA [grade point average], it's almost impossible to catch up."[23]

Entrance to medical school requires taking the Medical College Admissions Test. Most college students take this in the spring of their junior year or the fall of their senior year. The test measures knowledge of the sciences and ability to critically think, write, and

Premed students attend an anatomy class.

communicate. This exam, along with grades, personal recommendations, and an interview, is used to decide who is admitted to medical school. The interview is scheduled by the school and lasts from twenty minutes to an hour. The interviewers are usually medical school faculty members but can include a medical student from the school. Questions can range from asking the prospective student why he or she wants to attend that school to asking his or her opinion about a current medical dilemma, such as stem cell research.

Once a student is accepted into medical school, the curriculum is divided into two parts. For the first two years, students take advanced science courses like histology (the study of tissues), genetics (the study of patterns of inheritance), physiology (how the body works), and biochemistry (chemistry of living organisms). During this time, the student also learns to take medical histories and to perform patient examinations. The last two years of medical school concentrate on caring for patients in hospitals and clinics under the supervision of experienced doctors. These years are spent rotating through the various specialty areas to obtain a broad-based medical education. Medical students gain experience in all areas of practice, including pediatrics, surgery, family medicine, and psychiatry. Ninety-five to 98 percent of all medical school students graduate, despite long hours of classes, studying difficult subjects, and additional hours gaining experience at hospitals and clinics.

Specialization is obtained following graduation from medical school through a residency of three to seven years in the field in which the physician wishes to practice. This residency is a paid position of on-the-job training under the supervision of doctors who specialize in that area. Pediatrician Howard Scott is an example of a physician who helps with the education of residents. "I have students and resident physicians in my office continually, so I do lots of teaching."[24] Medical students must apply for a residency in a specialty area just as they applied to go to medical school. Osteopathic physicians practice in the same specialty areas as medical doctors, although about 45 percent of osteopaths choose family practice.

An example of a residency is one in pediatrics offered by Baylor College of Medicine. During this three-year residency, the physician, who already has a medical license, will be supervised while caring for newborns, working in clinics and hospitals caring for children, and learning about illnesses and injuries commonly seen in children in intensive care units or emergency rooms. Residents can

A Shortage of Minorities in Medical School

The American Association of Medical Colleges has identified some underrepresented minority groups in U.S. medical schools. These groups include blacks, Native Americans, Mexican Americans, and mainland Puerto Ricans. In 1999, out of a total enrollment of 67,000 medical students, only 4,267 were from these minority groups. Although this is a slight increase from previous years, the total is still lower than the medical colleges would prefer.

One of the strategies to increase minority enrollment is a program called the Minority Medical Education Program (MMEP). Instituted during the late 1980s, the MMEP offers summer educational experiences to promising, highly motivated minority students with the goal of helping them gain admission to medical schools. The programs are free, last for six weeks, and are open to students who have completed at least one year of college. Eleven medical schools in the United States offer this program. Each site plans its own curriculum, but most offer enrichment courses in math and science, preparation for the Medical College Admission Test, test-taking techniques, and a variety of clinical experiences with a physician-mentor.

spend from one to five months in each area during the three years. It is not uncommon for a resident to work eighty hours a week or have hospital duty for twenty-four hours straight.

After graduating from medical school, all physicians must be licensed by taking a national exam administered by the state in which they plan to work. Passing this examination is a requirement for employment as a doctor in the United States. In addition to a license, many physicians are certified by a physicians' specialty organization, such as one in pediatrics, family practice, or internal medicine. However, it is not necessary to have a certification to practice medicine. To qualify for certification, the physician must complete the required number of years of residency or work for one to two years in the field in which certification is desired. Following completion of a residency or this work experience, the physician takes a

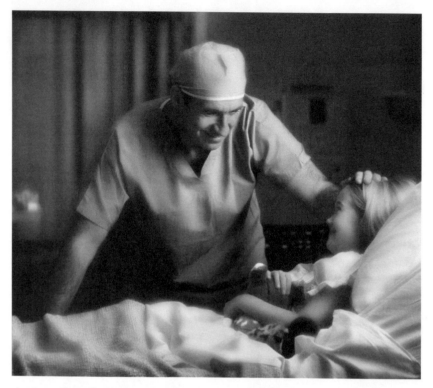

A *physician talks with a patient about her condition.*

certification examination to become a board-certified physician in the specialty area. The examination is a comprehensive one prepared by physicians who practice in that specialty.

Education does not end with the original medical school training but is a lifelong process. Medical knowledge constantly changes, and physicians must continue to take classes throughout their careers to remain current. This is essential so they can provide the most advanced, up-to-date treatments for their patients' conditions.

Office-Based Practices

Once a residency is completed, physicians can choose to work in a variety of settings. Although 20 percent of physicians work in hospitals as emergency room physicians, neonatologists (care of newborns), radiologists (studying X rays), or pathologists (studying cells and tissues to diagnose disease), about 70 percent of physicians choose an office-based practice.

Surgeons have office hours two or three days a week, but will spend more time in hospitals than other physicians, since they perform surgery there. Those physicians specializing in pediatrics, family practice, internal medicine, or psychiatry spend the majority of their time in the office, seeing patients by appointment, and only go to the hospital to visit patients. Doctors in the fields of radiology (X ray), pathology (laboratory testing), or anesthesiology may have offices in or near a hospital and spend the majority of their work-week at the hospital.

Physicians have the choice of working by themselves, known as private practice, or joining a group practice composed of several doctors working together in an office. Today more physicians are entering group practices, unlike the past, when the majority of physicians practiced alone. Many new physicians are prevented from setting up private practices because of the cost. Since 80 percent of physicians borrow money for their education, they are

Many physicians choose to work in an office-based practice.

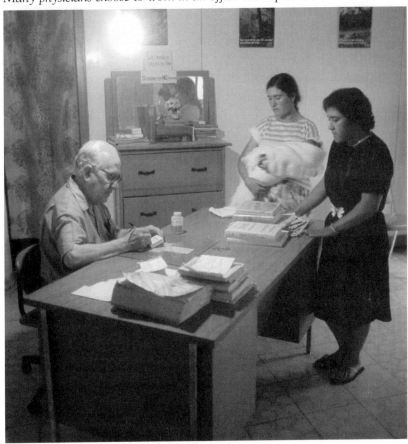

already in debt when they begin practice. Evan Provisor, a general surgeon in Connecticut, believes it is beneficial for new physicians to join a group practice with an established patient clientele because it shortens the time it takes to build a practice. "Very few doctors set up practice on their own right out of residency. It's a big hassle with a lot of insecurity and no guaranteed income."[25]

The trend toward group practice allows doctors to share weekend, holiday, and on-call duty and the administrative duties of running an office. A group practice puts a physician in contact with other professionals on a daily basis. Susan Breen, an ophthalmologist at a clinic in Massachusetts, says, "One of the benefits of being in a group practice was that if I had a very tough case, I could ask my colleagues down the hall for advice."[26]

Many physicians prefer to establish a private practice rather than work with a group of physicians. For physicians who practice alone, the independence of running their own practice is an important consideration and is one of the factors in their original decision to choose a medical career. Kenneth Callen, a psychiatrist in Washington State, comments, "There were multiple factors [in his decision to become a doctor], but the sense of independence was most important."[27] Working alone offers the physician the opportunity to build the type of practice desired. In addition, private practice offers the best opportunity to increase income once a physician becomes established since physicians who work in group practices often work for a set salary.

Other Opportunities

Although most physicians work in offices or hospitals, government agencies such as the Centers for Disease Control, the National Institutes of Health, and the Food and Drug Administration also employ doctors. John Coulehan tells about his year as the only physician for an Indian Health Service office:

> I'd frequently see seventy to eighty patients in a day, some of whom were very sick, some of whom just rode into town to socialize a few hours and pick up a new bottle of "big red pills" for their aches and pains. There were days I'd walk home lightly in the evening with my heart singing, "This is the life for me!" There were also days on which I'd walk home feeling incompetent, overworked, and overwhelmed.[28]

Female Physicians

According to the American Medical Association, female physicians represented slightly over 20 percent of all practicing physicians in the United States in 1996. This number is four times greater than the number of female doctors in 1970. In 1997 the total number of women graduating from medical schools in the United States was 6,614.

In 1849 Elizabeth Blackwell was the first woman in the United States to earn a medical degree. Blackwell's entrance into the field of medicine encouraged other women; just ten years later three hundred women in the United States had earned medical degrees. Still, prejudice against women enrolled in medical schools persisted until the early 1970s, when federal regulations barred medical schools from limiting the number of females accepted to their programs.

In spite of the limited number of women accepted into medical schools, female physicians have made important contributions to medicine. In 1952 Dr. Virginia Apgar devised a scoring system for assessing the health of newborns, and in 1944 Dr. Helen Brook Taussig invented a surgical procedure for babies with heart defects. Another woman, Dr. Nancy W. Dickey, was elected as the first female president of the American Medical Association in 1997.

A woman physician at work.

At present the largest percentage of female physicians practice internal medicine or pediatrics. Fewer women choose the higher-paying fields of surgery or anesthesiology, thus making their annual income lower than the average for male physicians.

The future is bright for female physicians. It is anticipated that by the year 2010, 30 percent of all U.S. physicians will be women.

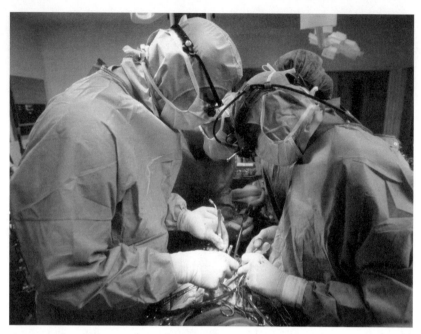

A team of surgeons performs heart surgery.

Physicians who specialize in working in public health do not work with individual patients but rather consider the needs of the community as a whole when looking at health problems. They work on preventive measures to help the public deal with illnesses like tuberculosis and sexually transmitted diseases. They also focus on potential health issues like unsafe drinking water, teenage pregnancy, and statistics and programs related to smoking. Instead of taking an individual patient history, they survey communities to gather information that will help in planning health needs for a city or county.

Some physicians spend all or part of their careers as military doctors. Military service offers opportunities to work in many of the same specialties that are available in civilian life. Howard Scott served for two years in the army as a pediatrician before setting up his own practice. Kenneth Callen served as a psychiatrist in the air force. The military appeals to some doctors because they have programs available to help new physicians repay some of the cost of their medical education.

Professional Advancement

Physicians can advance professionally in several ways. Most physicians advance by expanding their practice or by building a good reputation. Once a new doctor becomes established in a community, other physicians may send patients to the newer doctor if he or she becomes known as a competent specialist. Another way physicians enlarge their practice is by recommendations from satisfied patients.

Teaching at a university is also a way to become recognized. Both Callen and Scott have held faculty positions at medical schools. A physician teaching at a medical school lectures on diseases or supervises student doctors as they care for patients in hospitals and clinics. Teaching allows a physician to stay current on new treatments and technologies since most medical schools are part of large medical centers where research on diseases and treatments is conducted.

Some physicians, employed by laboratories or university medical schools, conduct research and can become respected experts by publishing their findings. Examples of areas in which research is conducted are childhood asthma or new treatments for cancer. Physicians begin testing new treatments on laboratory animals. If the treatment is a success, the next step is called a clinical trial, during which the treatment is used on patients who volunteer for the research study and who have signed an informed consent form.

Another way to advance is through further education, following a residency, in one of twenty-two subspecialties. A physician who has completed a residency in internal medicine, a field covering many medical diseases, may decide to have a practice limited to blood disorders. In order to do this, the physician takes a one- to two-year course in hematology, which is the subspecialty that focuses on diseases of the blood. Other subspecialty choices for physicians in internal medicine are diabetes, arthritis, or cardiology, which concentrates on diseases of the heart. Some physicians advance by obtaining additional college degrees in microbiology or biochemistry.

Salaries for Physicians

The amount of education necessary to become a physician and the great responsibility they have accounts for physicians' higher-than-average income. A survey taken in 2000 by Physician Search says the national average income for a first-year physician in primary care (family practice, internal medicine, or pediatrics) is between $115,000 and $125,000. After three or more years in practice, the same group averaged $145,000 to $150,000 a year.

Although physicians are listed as one of the highest-paid occupations, the amount of money earned depends on their specialty.

Specialists who earn the most are radiologists, anesthesiologists, and surgeons. Their annual earnings are between $217,000 and $260,000. These specialties require approximately five years in residency training beyond medical school, compared to three years for primary care physicians. Physicians who are completing their specialty education during a residency are paid between $34,000 and $42,000 per year while working under the direct supervision of an experienced physician in that specialty.

Physicians who are self-employed make more money than those in group practices who receive salaries. Private practice physicians can increase their earnings by receiving fees from each individual patient rather than by receiving a set salary for all patients seen, as is common in a group practice. Factors that determine income for private-practice physicians, in addition to the physician's specialty, are the number of hours worked; the reputation, skill, and personality of the physician; and the geographic area in which the practice is located. Personality helps a physician build a practice because patients prefer to see a doctor who is friendly and shows interest and concern for their problems. Physicians in or near cities and large medical centers tend to earn more money than doctors who practice in rural areas where the opportunities to build a large practice are limited.

Physicians in the Twenty-First Century

Job opportunities for physicians will remain readily available during the twenty-first century, although a physician oversupply occurred during the last half of the twentieth century. A May 2001 article in *Medical Student Journal of the American Medical Association* presents several viewpoints related to the physician oversupply. One viewpoint is that the current health care system in the United States creates limited opportunities for practice. An opposite opinion is that positions are not equally filled since rural areas have openings. Still another viewpoint, indicating a need for more physicians, is that public demand for physicians has not lessened.

Regardless of the reason for the oversupply, future physicians can expect shorter working hours and earlier retirement, which will create more job openings. The *Occupational Outlook Handbook* says that employment of physicians will grow faster than average for all occupations through the year 2008. There are two reasons suggested for this increase. One reason is the growing number of elderly people in the United States who need medical care. The second reason is that more diseases are now treatable than in the past and new technologies are available to use as treatment.

In addition, the number of future physician jobs will vary according to the part of the country and whether the location is rural or urban. The greatest number of future positions for physicians will occur in rural areas or low-income areas, which often have more difficulty recruiting physicians because of poor medical facilities or limited income opportunities. The northeastern and western parts of the United States and urban areas currently have the most doctors per patient population. Family physicians, pediatricians, and those in internal medicine often have good job prospects because they are the physicians who see patients first and who refer patients to other specialists.

There are numerous reasons to consider a career as a physician during the twenty-first century. The position has always been a rewarding one, not only financially but also personally and intellectually. Dr. Howard Scott says, "There are many advantages and few disadvantages [to being a physician]. It's a great career—likely the best. Very likely no other profession is able to give you as much self-satisfaction and joy. If I had it to do over again—I'd do the same thing."[29]

Chapter 3

Medical Technologists

Medical technologists pursue the unknown in search of clues that will help physicians diagnose illnesses. They do this by examining specimens of body fluids, tissues, or cells for abnormalities. Joyce McCalmon Jones, Kansas, a medical technologist certified by the American Society of Clinical Pathologists (ASCP), says,

> What I especially like about my area is the challenge of pursuing the unknown. As one begins testing specimens, there is always the prospect of discovering something out of the norm that can be helpful in a diagnosis. I really do like my job as a mystery scientist; trying to solve and see what's behind the squeaky door. [30]

Medical technologists are also known as clinical laboratory technologists and, more recently, as laboratory scientists to differentiate them from emergency medical technicians, who have a similar-sounding professional name. They are the third largest health care profession, after nurses and physicians. In a book published in 1999 by Les Krantz on the best jobs, positions in medical technology ranked 16 out of 250 jobs surveyed. This was based on salary, stress level, work environment, outlook, security, and physical demands.

Although many people are interested in working in the field of medicine, not everyone wants direct contact with the sick. "Being a medical laboratory technologist is a good profession for someone who wants to help people, but who doesn't want to be around sick people all the time," [31] says Carolyn West, director of a vocational-technical school in Wichita, Kansas. Technologists work mostly in laboratories and have limited patient contact, except for occasions when they draw blood specimens.

Mystery Scientist

In pursuing the unknown, medical technologists examine and analyze specimens from patients sent to the lab for diagnostic purposes. Laboratory workers perform tests that play a crucial role in detection, diagnosis, and treatment of disease. It is the responsibility of medical technologists to confirm the accuracy of test results, whether done by themselves or done by automation, and report these to the patient's physician. Some of the types of specimens that technologists examine are blood, urine, sputum, feces, spinal fluid, and cell or tissue samples. Using these specimens from patients, a medical technologist can check for diseases that range from anemia and parasite invasions to AIDS, diabetes, or cancer.

Technologists use many types of equipment, including microscopes, which identify bacteria or abnormal cells in a specimen. Computers, precision instruments such as cell counters, and complex

A medical technologist performs a diagnostic test in a laboratory.

electronic equipment, which can automatically analyze specimens, check for amounts of normal or abnormal chemicals in the body and screen blood and urine for the presence of legally or illegally prescribed drugs. Technologists may also be involved in training technicians who work with them or student technologists who are assigned to their lab to gain necessary experience prior to graduation.

Technologists working in small labs perform many types of tests. Those who work in large labs have an opportunity to specialize in one area of clinical laboratory testing. The five major areas of a lab in which technologists work are blood banks, chemistry, hematology, immunology, and microbiology, also called bacteriology. Blood bank technologists prepare units of blood for transfusion by running tests to ensure the blood will not cause an adverse reaction in the person receiving it. Nalita Bali, a medical technologist, works in biochemistry. "I analyze chemicals in the blood and mainly use high-tech equipment to diagnose a range of diseases such as liver failure and diabetes. We also do tests for genetic diseases."[32] Hematology technologists check red and white blood cells and platelets for number, size, and shape. Immunology technologists specialize in the immune system of the body, and microbiology technologists identify microorganisms that can cause disease. A final group of laboratory workers are cytotechnologists, who prepare slides of body cells to be examined under the microscope.

The Three Ps: Preciseness, Problem-Solving, Pressure

A key characteristic of medical technologists is the ability to do precise work since the results of lab tests influence how a physician diagnoses and treats an illness. A small change in lab results could affect patient care, so attention to detail and the ability to do accurate, reliable work is a requirement. Patients taking medication to prevent clots from forming in their blood need frequent blood tests so that the physician can order the correct dose of medication. If the technologist fails to accurately perform the test, the patient could receive a dose of medication that is too high or too low. Medical technologists must recognize when lab results are incorrect so they can retest the specimens or correct the results. Regarding newer machines used in the lab, Jones says, "The computer will tell you if there is a big difference in a patient's test

What Is a Phlebotomist?

A phlebotomist is a person employed by a clinical lab and trained to draw blood. The name *phlebotomist* comes from the Greek word *phlebo*, which means vein. Phlebotomists learn the art of locating veins and piercing the skin with a needle to obtain specimens of blood. Specimens are then tested for abnormalities by a technologist.

Phlebotomists have the most patient contact of any lab personnel. Some qualifications are that they must like people and be friendly, be able to work quickly, have good vision to help them locate veins, and be able to read lab slips, which contain information about needed specimens. They then must use this information to obtain the correct amount of blood and put it in the proper tube.

Phlebotomists are employed in hospitals, clinics, neighborhood health centers, and group practices. Most phlebotomists receive on-the-job training. There are a small number of formal training programs available at colleges and hospitals around the country, which usually last a few months. The average salary of a phlebotomist is $17,000 per year or $9.90 an hour.

A patient winces as a phlebotomist draws blood.

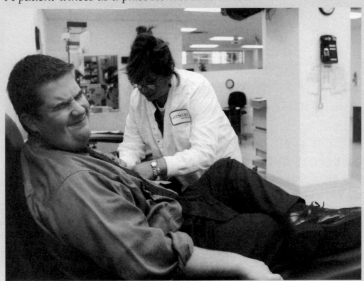

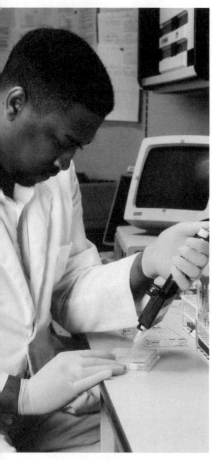

A lab technologist performs a test on a tissue sample.

results from previous values, but it is also important for the technologist to know theory which tells you when lab values fall outside the normal range."[33]

The ability to use information from lab tests to solve problems is a common characteristic of those who choose the profession. Technologists must be able to use charts, tables, books, or other facts to make decisions. Jones says she had a situation in which the nursing staff questioned unusual lab values written on a lab slip by another technologist. Jones had to use her knowledge to decide if these values were correct. In this instance, it was only a matter of the technologist writing the results in the wrong column. Medical technologists have an interest in discovering solutions to diagnostic problems. Jones says a good technologist will "use logic to arrive at the conclusions, and good common sense!"[34]

Lab technologists should be able to work under pressure. In addition to a normal workload, technologists often receive specimens from patients who are in a medical crisis, such as a heart attack. The specimens are delivered to the lab with instructions to perform a test stat, which means the physician wants the results immediately to help make a diagnosis.

Performing the tests requires manual dexterity and normal color vision. Technologists often visually inspect specimens for color and clarity or the presence of microscopic amounts of blood. Color changes in specimens can also indicate bacteria growth or a higher-than-normal level of a substance such as glucose. Manual dexterity is necessary for handling the complex and intricate equipment. Sometimes lack of manual dexterity can also cause "sloppy technique,"[35] says Jones. Preparing blood transfusions requires adding drops of a solution to blood samples. "I worked with a technologist who didn't drop the solution, but added it by squirts. This can affect the results."[36]

In performing some of the tests, there may be unpleasant odors because of the nature of the specimens and the chemicals that technologists are exposed to on a daily basis. For those people sensitive to odors, this could be a major disadvantage.

In addition to unpleasant odors, technologists may be exposed to infectious agents in the specimens they examine and must follow all safety requirements. Specimens may contain dangerous bacteria or viruses. Anyone working in a lab receives thorough training on protecting themselves from exposure to infected body fluids. Gloves, goggles, and hand washing are part of standard precautions used.

Many laboratory scientists spend long hours standing on their feet. This means that those considering this career must be in good physical condition in order to withstand fatigue. The amount of standing depends on how the lab is set up and the area of the lab in which the person works. Some specialties, like chemistry, require more standing than areas of the lab where technologists sit while using microscopes.

Laboratory technologists must be available to work days, evenings, or nights, and must also work on some holidays and weekends. Laboratories in hospitals must be staffed twenty-four hours a day, seven days a week. Some technologists may have to be on call for emergencies. This means that they could be called into work from home if the lab gets very busy.

A Science-Based Education

To become a medical technologist, one must earn a bachelor's degree in medical technology or clinical laboratory science or a degree in a life science, such as chemistry or microbiology. Essential college courses are chemistry, biological sciences, microbiology, mathematics, and specialized courses that teach skills used in clinical laboratories. Jones says, "I would not recommend this profession to anybody who is not interested in science."[37] Some programs also include management, business, and computer application programs. Clinical experience, in which students work in all areas of the lab, is an essential part of training.

In the past, an alternate educational route combined formal training and work experience. Completion of a two- or three-year college program in medical technology or science and a twelve-month period of supervised practical training allowed students to qualify for positions as medical technologists. A four-year college degree is now required.

Certification in medical technology is offered through professional organizations after passing an examination. Hiring a certified technologist assures the employer that the technologist has the theory and knowledge necessary to obtain accurate results on a wide range of laboratory tests. The ASCP Board of Registry offers certification to individuals who have completed academic courses, clinical laboratory education or experience, and who have successfully passed a computerized examination. Passing a certification exam given by the ASCP allows technologists to use the initials MT (ASCP) after their names, which shows that they are recognized as qualified in the field.

A technologist can be certified as a generalist, meaning the technologist has received education in all areas of lab work. This is the type of certification usually obtained immediately following graduation. Technologists can also obtain specialty certification in a field of their choice, at a later time. Although certification is voluntary, it is a prerequisite for many jobs and is often necessary for advancement. Other organizations offering certification are the American Medical Technologists, the National Certification Agency for Medical Laboratory Personnel, and the Credentialing Commission of the International Society for Clinical Laboratory Technology.

In addition to certification through occupational licensing boards, some states require that technologists be licensed or registered. Requirements for licensure are not always the same but they nearly always include a written examination. For example, the state of Tennessee will issue a license following proof that the applicant has passed one of the national certification examinations.

Job Opportunities

Employment prospects for technologists are anticipated to grow about as fast as the average for all occupations through 2008, according to the *Occupational Outlook Handbook*. There are several trends that affect job growth. As with other health professions, the rapidly growing elderly population, which is more likely to have long-term diseases that require monitoring with lab tests, is increasing the number of laboratory diagnostic tests being done.

The History of Medical Technology

The beginnings of medical technology can be traced back to ancient times. In fact, urine analysis was the first diagnostic test done. In 600 B.C. a physician discovered that diabetics excreted sugar in their urine by actually tasting the urine.

Several centuries later (1763), Antoni van Leeuwenhoek invented an important diagnostic tool—the first usable microscope. The microscope allowed important advances to be made in the examination of blood, other body fluids, and tissues by making abnormalities that were not apparent to the human eye visible. The microscope is still an important piece of laboratory equipment today.

By the last half of the nineteenth century a few hospitals in the United States had clinical laboratories. World War I (1914–1918) increased the demand for laboratories in both military and civilian hospitals as the value of laboratory testing to aid diagnosis was recognized. By 1920, there were thirty-five hundred technicians working, a little over half of them women.

Until 1921 laboratory workers were mainly nurses, or even secretaries, who were trained by the physician who employed them. The first formal laboratory course was held in Philadelphia in 1921–1922. The University of Minnesota was the first school to offer a degree in medical technology, setting the standard for the training of technologists in a university setting.

In 1922 the American Society of Clinical Pathologists was organized to promote education in the profession so that standards of laboratory science would improve. Another stated goal of the organization was the improvement of public health. Today the society offers certification examinations for technologists as proof of their competence, in addition to serving as their professional organization.

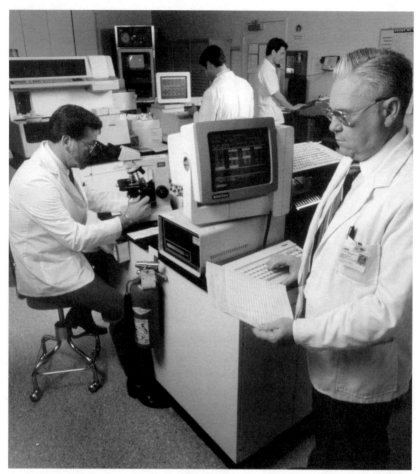

Automated equipment performs many tests once done by technologists.

Although newly developed laboratory tests are causing doctors to order more tests, automation and simpler tests allow fewer employees to do the work. Research has simplified many testing processes so that nonprofessional laboratory people—and even patients—are able to perform many specimen examinations, such as blood sugar testing for diabetes. Advanced automation allows machines to prepare specimens, a job formerly done by technologists. Automated machines are able to take as little as one-half of a teaspoon of blood and run as many as twenty tests simultaneously.

Despite these technological advances, the ASCP has reported that vacancy rates in jobs for the year 2000 for medical technology staff members is 11.1 percent, which is an increase of nearly 3 percent from 1996. There is also an increase in unfilled positions for supervisors. Recently, there has been a shortage of students entering the profession. Jones expresses the opinion that "many are not choosing this field because the chances for advancement are limited and the use of automation has made the field less challenging."[38] Because of the number of unfilled positions, many part-time jobs are available for those wanting to work but not wanting a full-time job. One out of five laboratory personnel works part-time. Part-time work in a lab is available to students while they are in school and also to graduate medical technologists. The shortage of medical technologists mirrors the need for workers found in most other health care professions.

Medical technologists can be employed in a variety of settings, including hospitals, independent labs, public health services, research facilities, and physicians' offices. Half of all laboratory technologists work in hospitals. Jobs for hospital-based technologists are expected to experience a slower growth due to the number of medical conditions currently treated on an outpatient basis. For this same reason, jobs in offices and clinics will increase more rapidly. Independent medical laboratories performing tests for hospitals and doctors' offices will experience the fastest growth. Government positions are also available at the Department of Veterans Affairs, the U.S. Public Health Services, and the Centers for Disease Control. Only a small number of technologists work in regional blood banks and research or testing laboratories.

Crime labs are another area in which technologists work. Technologists working in crime labs examine and evaluate evidence collected at the scene of a crime. This evidence could include blood, body secretions or tissues, fingerprints, or screening for use of illegal drugs and alcohol. Blood or a single hair root found at the scene of a crime can be tested using DNA technology (which makes up the composition of genes that determine inherited characteristics) to identify a person since everyone's DNA is different.

Professional Advancement

Technologists interested in advancing can become supervisors or managers of a laboratory. A master's degree in medical technology increases chances for advancement. Teaching positions in the field of medical technology require a master's degree or a doctorate, in addition to experience in the field. Master's degrees in medical technology are needed for those interested in administration or research.

Likewise, advanced degrees can prepare a person for work in highly specialized laboratory work such as genetics. Becoming a specialist in one area of laboratory work is another avenue to advancement. A doctorate is usually needed to become a laboratory director, except in the case of smaller labs, which do not perform extremely complex procedures.

Manufacturers of laboratory equipment and supplies often hire technologists with experience to help develop or market products or to work in sales. These manufacturers use the services of technologists to give valuable advice about what kind of blood analyzers and other automated machines engineers need to design. Technologists are also employed by manufacturers to train hospital and clinic personnel how to use new equipment. Positions with manufacturers usually pay more than labs that provide direct health care services. Linda Jones, a laboratory manager in Virginia, says, "About half of the graduates of a nearby medical technology program aren't going into hospital jobs. They're going to work at pharmaceutical companies or in sales positions where they can make much higher salaries."[39]

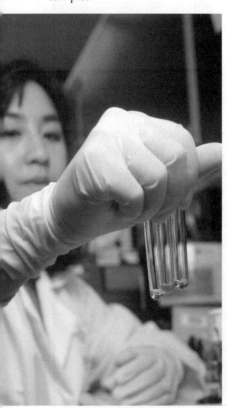

A technologist compares blood samples.

Salaries for Medical Technologists

Salaries for medical technologists depend on the amount of experience and the job setting. Yearly salaries for experienced technologists range from $35,000 to $50,820. The average salary for a beginning technologist is approximately $27,000 a year. A survey done by the ASCP in 2000 showed the average hourly wage for all medical technology staff employees to be $17.90. Supervisors made $21.50 an hour, and managers earned $27.00 per hour.

The ASCP surveyed technologists working in specialty areas in

Some Laboratory Tests

When specimens of body fluids are sent to a laboratory, technologists perform a variety of tests depending on the specimen and the physician's requests. Modern laboratories are equipped to perform many types of analyses. The technologist performs some tests manually, and some are completed using automation.

In one blood test, the number of red blood cells, white blood cells, and platelets are counted and compared to normal values for each. Abnormal numbers could indicate anemia, infection, inflammation, leukemia, or a blood-clotting problem, depending on which of the three cells examined shows a problem. These cells are also checked microscopically for size and shape and whether they are mature or immature.

Patients taking certain prescribed drugs for heart problems, seizures, chronic breathing problems, and some mental disorders need to have the levels of these drugs in their blood checked so that toxic symptoms do not develop. Periodically the physician orders a blood sample drawn so that the amount of the medication in the patient's body can be compared to known safe limits. The results are used to adjust medication dosages.

Laboratory scientists check urine for the presence of abnormal substances, such as blood, glucose, and protein. A simple test for these involves dipping a chemical strip into the urine; the strip changes color in the presence of these substances. Laboratory scientists can also perform microscopic examinations on urine to determine the presence of bacteria, which cause infections. In addition, urine samples and other body fluids can be placed in special substances to check for the growth of colonies of bacteria—a process known as a culture.

Laboratory tests are very important to good medical care. Many diseases could not be detected without the knowledge of laboratory scientists using specialized tests and equipment to aid the physician in diagnosing illnesses.

A technologist reviews test results on a computer. Computer skills are essential for this work.

1998 and published the following findings: cytotechnologists in staff positions averaged between $18.70 and $19.30 an hour; histologic technologists averaged between $14.00 and $15.70 an hour. Private labs paid less in both categories than hospitals.

Areas of the United States that pay higher salaries for both medical technology staff and supervisory positions are the far West and the Northeast. In both areas, costs of living are higher, requiring greater salaries.

Medical Technology in the Twenty-First Century

The field of laboratory science is constantly changing. In the future, workers in this field must keep their skills current because of new areas of testing, such as DNA. Another continuing trend is the use of more computerized and automated equipment, including robots that can prepare some specimens, a job now performed by technologists. Procedures that formerly required technologists to perform multiple steps are being completed by automation with the touch of a button. Everything from receiving samples to reporting results can be done with automation or robots. Other steps that can be accomplished include sorting tubes, removing their rubber stoppers, centrifuging them (spinning the contents to cause settling of heavier parts of the specimen), and loading the test tubes into blood analyzers. Test tubes can be bar coded for identification similar to groceries. Large numbers of tests can be done quickly and inexpensively because of the new technology. As a result, future technologists will use their expertise to analyze the accuracy of test results that are done automatically or by robots. Knowledge of computer technology will be essential.

Nevertheless, a survey done by the American Society for Medical Technology found that 60 percent of states have reported a shortage of technologists. The Bureau of Labor Statistics is anticipating an increase in the number of jobs for medical technologists by 10 to 20 percent through 2008. An article in the July 2001 *Denver Business Journal* indicated a severe shortage of workers in the Denver area. According to Stuart Pritchard, director of HealthOne's North Suburban Medical Center, "Right now for my lab I'm OK, but the last time I had to place an ad for a medical technologist, I did not even get a response for three months. If I were to lose a person right now, I would be in the same boat."[40]

Chapter 4

Physical Therapists

Physical therapists are the rehabilitation specialists in the field of medicine. Therapists provide a service whose aim is to restore people to their optimum level of functioning following injury or illness. Injuries range from low back pain to motor vehicle accidents, and illnesses can include heart disease and arthritis. The therapist tests each patient and designs a program of treatment that will accomplish the goals of improving functioning and relieving pain.

The field of physical therapy has been growing, particularly since World War II. During the 1940s physical therapy achieved great results in treating those injured in battle. Since then many advances have been made that have changed the outcome for those with conditions that affect daily functioning. Today, the career offers many job opportunities and performs a valuable service in the rehabilitation of patients with certain illnesses and injuries.

Working for Recovery

To rehabilitate a patient, physical therapists set a specific goal, such as restoring mobility. Part of working with patients is developing an individualized plan of care. Therapists' clients suffer from a wide range of conditions resulting from accidents, birth defects, and medical problems, and their clientele can include the very young or the very old. Although the goal of treatment is to restore the patient to the highest level of functioning that he or she is capable of attaining given the injury or illness, the method of reaching the goal may vary. Even people who have the same illness or injury may respond differently to therapy due to age, previous physical conditions, pre-existing health problems, or their motivation. Good therapists would use a different approach for an eighty-year-old patient with a broken leg than for an eighteen-year-old recovering from the same injury. Patients who are referred for physical therapy come to therapy with instructions from a physician. These instructions can be very specific, telling the therapist exactly what the physician wants done, or they can be very general, saying "evaluate and treat," thus leaving the type of treatment to the physical therapist's discretion. Using the physician's information and the patient's medical history, the therapist performs tests to measure muscle strength and compares the results to normal values. Joints are measured for range of motion, and activities are observed that determine coordination.

Two of the treatments that therapists prescribe to rehabilitate patients are whirlpool baths and exercises. One of the uses for whirlpool baths is cleaning burns prior to redressing them. Exercise prescriptions are used following knee or shoulder surgery to restore full range of motion. Therapists also are responsible for teaching patients how to safely use walkers or crutches, which assist them with moving. Following a stroke, a patient may be weak and have a problem with balance and will be taught how to correctly use a walker.

Therapists use a variety of techniques in treating patients. One treatment method involves performing passive exercises by using

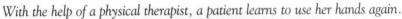

With the help of a physical therapist, a patient learns to use her hands again.

their hands to guide the muscles of the patient through range-of-motion exercises when the patient is physically unable to do so. This keeps the muscles strong until the patient is capable of performing the exercises without assistance. Physical therapists also know how to set up traction on a hospital bed when it is needed to hold fractured bones in proper alignment. In some cases, physical therapists are responsible for wound treatment and for dressing changes for those with pressure sores, which result from lying on one part of the body too long, or external ulcers, which are caused by poor circulation or injury.

In addition to rehabilitating patients, physical therapists work with nurses and other health care workers in a preventive role. Therapists are the experts in a hospital on correct lifting and moving techniques for patients. Since back injuries are an occupational hazard for those caring for bedridden patients, physical therapists often teach other employees how to avoid painful injuries when moving patients.

The teaching duties of a therapist frequently extend to the patient and the patient's family. Once a patient is discharged from a treatment program, exercises and relaxation practices are continued at home. According to therapist Laurie DeJong, "We do a lot of education in terms of posture and how patients can prevent injuries from recurring."[41] The physical therapist teaches the family to provide emotional support or actual assistance with therapies.

Using Patience and Motivation

Working with sick and injured patients with the goal of rehabilitation requires many qualities in a physical therapist. Qualities needed include personal physical fitness, patience, and the ability to encourage others. DeJong says, "You have to really love working with people and have to possess a great deal of patience. Change and improvement don't happen overnight. Often the person you're working with is impatient to get better, but you have to be the steadying force."[42]

Good health and physical fitness are necessary not only because therapists are frequently involved with lifting, moving, and supporting weakened patients but also because therapists need to set a good example for patients and other health care workers who might find it difficult to follow the advice of someone who is not a good role model. In addition to possessing good health, therapists must be able

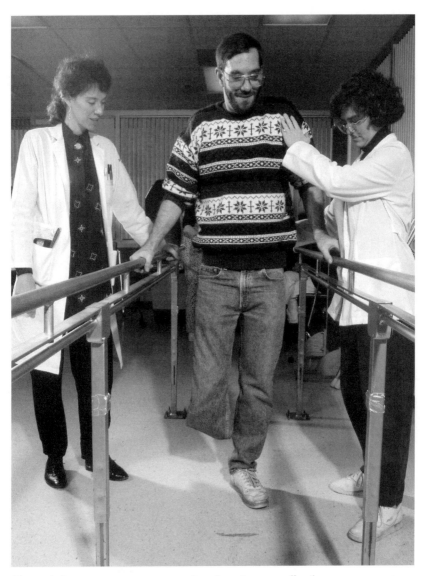

Physical therapists encourage a patient learning to walk after an amputation.

to work with their hands, which are used to massage and move parts of the body.

However, the physical demands of the job can be challenging. Therapists must be in good enough physical condition to lift, kneel, stoop, or stand for long periods. They are sometimes required to move heavy equipment and must be strong enough to help patients turn, stand, and walk. Kelly Bartek, a physical therapy coordinator, worked in an acute care hospital for two years before changing to an outpatient clinic specializing in the care of patients recovering from bone and muscle injuries and surgery. She has this to say about the physical aspects of hospital work versus her current job: "When I worked at the hospital, I was doing lots of lifting, lots of transferring, and gait training [teaching correct walking] with patients. It was a much more physically demanding job when you have a physically weak and debilitated population."[43] Even though therapists receive extensive training in lifting and moving techniques, back injuries can still be an occupational hazard.

The ability to continue to motivate a patient and remain positive and persuasive is an essential characteristic of a successful therapist. Progress is often slow following illnesses like strokes, the loss of an arm or leg, or spinal cord injuries, and a good physical therapist demonstrates patience. Many clients become depressed following ill-

Physical Therapy Assistants and Aides

Physical therapists are often assisted in their work by licensed physical therapy assistants or by physical therapy aides. A physical therapy assistant has graduated from a two-year program with an associate degree. Most of these programs have waiting lists for admission. Like physical therapists, assistants study science, psychology, and math and have clinical experience as part of their course of study. Physical therapy assistants also must pass a licensing exam. They provide much of a patient's treatment, all under the supervision of a licensed physical therapist who has evaluated the patient and has designed a therapy program.

Physical therapy aides work under the supervision of a physical therapist or a physical therapist assistant. Requirements to be an aide include graduation from high school and a desire to work with people. On-the-job training is usually provided by the agency employing them. Aides are responsible for setting up equipment, transporting patients, assisting patients with ambulation (walking), answering the phone, and ordering supplies.

Average pay for an assistant or aide in a hospital is $21,200 per year, with the lower end of the pay scale at $13,000 per year.

nesses in which they lose the ability to either care for themselves or to function at their previous level. Bartek says,

> A lot of times they just want someone to understand that they are in pain and hurting and that this is affecting their life, and we can be there for them and it is rewarding. There is a lot they are dealing with psychologically as well as their injury. Some of them are off work, and a lot of their identity is related to their work, and they are scared about losing their job. You can't just say do these exercises and leave it at that. You kind of have to treat the whole person. [44]

The satisfaction of seeing improvement in a patient's level of functioning is one of the main advantages. Jeff Littmann, a physical therapist for the Institute for Rehabilitation and Research in Houston, says that patients are what recharge him on his job: "Seeing them progress and learn new skills is reward enough." [45]

Difficult Entrance Requirements

Having the necessary personal characteristics is not enough to gain entrance into a physical therapy program. Entrance requirements for physical therapy programs are some of the most rigorous of any health care field. There are several reasons for this. One reason is that the programs take a limited number of applicants because of a shortage of qualified instructors, who must have either a doctorate or a master's degree plus several years' experience. Another reason for the rigid entrance requirements is that the program lasts six years and is difficult, so schools want to make sure applicants are intellectually able to master the courses. A third reason is that the professional organizations for physical therapists want to keep the quality of graduates high. Students must have excellent grades in high school and early college, particularly in the sciences and math.

Due to competition for entry into physical therapy programs, candidates must meet high standards set by screening committees. Although there were 189 accredited physical therapy programs in 1999, most schools only graduate twenty to forty students per year. This is in part because of the shortage of qualified instructors and the need for close supervision of students as they care for patients. In addition to superior grades, many schools require applicants to complete up to 150 hours of volunteer activities in a physical therapy setting. Some schools also interview applicants as a way of choosing the

The Licensing Exam for Physical Therapists

All physical therapists must pass a licensing exam. Therapists take a national examination once they have graduated from an accredited school of physical therapy. The computerized examination lasts four-and-a-half hours and consists of 225 multiple-choice questions. Some states require a demonstration of skills in addition to the exam.

Candidates approved by the state-licensing agency to take the exam receive an "authorization-to-test" letter and must take the exam within sixty days of that time. It is the responsibility of the candidate to schedule an exam at one of the testing centers located in large cities in each state.

Candidates who fail the exam are given additional opportunities to pass. The number of opportunities to retest varies by area of the country, but no one is allowed to take the examination more than four times in one year. In 1999–2000, the pass rate for students in the United States, taking the exam for the first time, was 77.78 percent.

best students. They are interested in how well an applicant conducts him or herself during the interview, according to Bartek. However, they also want to know about involvement in health-related clubs at school to determine whether the prospective student shows leadership qualities.

In the past, most physical therapy programs required a four- to six-year college education that led to a degree in physical therapy. Accredited programs currently are eliminating their four-year programs in favor of a six-year one that leads to a master's degree in physical therapy. The first two years concentrate on science courses, including biology, chemistry, and physics. Courses in psychology are included because therapists must know how to motivate patients while remaining sensitive to personal problems. The final years offer more specialized courses, such as neuroanatomy, the study of the body's nervous system, and biomechanics, the application of mechanical principles such as moving and lifting. Students are taught how to evaluate patients and design treatments for specific diseases. Supervised clinical experience by a licensed therapist employed at hospitals and outpatient settings is also part of the education.

All states require physical therapists to be licensed in order to work. To qualify for the exam, physical therapy students have to demonstrate the ability to perform the required skills before graduation. These skills might include setting up traction, performing range-of-motion exercises, teaching a patient to use crutches, or demonstrating muscle-strengthening exercises. Eligibility requirements for a license include graduation from an accredited physical therapy program. A few states require a student to demonstrate competence on physical therapy skills as part of the licensing examination. Once graduates pass the examination, they are known as physical therapists and use the initials *PT* after their names.

Most states require physical therapists to attend continuing education seminars in order to be eligible for license renewal. According to Bartek, in Texas, where she practices, she is required to attend thirty hours of classes every two years. These classes keep therapists current in their field since treatments change as the result of new technology. Examples of continuing education classes are aquatic physical therapy, electrical stimulation for chronic wounds, and rehabilitation of amputees.

Many Job Opportunities

The *Occupational Outlook Handbook* predicts that employment opportunities in physical therapy will grow faster than the average for all occupations, with the majority of new jobs becoming available after 2003. Bartek says,

> There used to be almost a dire shortage of physical thera-pists. With the changes in health care, there is not nearly the demand. You are probably not going to get your first [job] choice. It has changed a little bit. It is more on the rebound now. Jobs are becoming a little more available. When there was a shortage, a lot of schools opened up.[46]

For those seeking employment, hospitals and physical therapy offices offer almost two-thirds of the available jobs in the field. Other areas where jobs are available are home health, nursing homes, rehabilitation centers, and physician-run clinics. A therapist can work with a wide variety of clients, ranging from a pediatric population in a children's hospital to the elderly in a nursing home. The services of therapists are needed for medical conditions like heart problems or strokes. Some therapists choose to specialize in the care of burns; others prefer working in a sports medicine facility treating sports-related injuries. Therapists, who desire a variety of conditions in a workday, can be employed in a general hospital setting that will offer most of the conditions mentioned.

Those who like more independence may choose home health or self-employment. Self-employed therapists work in private practice. They provide services for a fee to hospitals, nursing homes, home health agencies, or schools. In schools, therapists are hired by the school district to work with children who have developmental delays. For example, a child with cerebral palsy or spina bifida, which is a birth defect involving the spine, may have trouble walking. "I like working with the kids because I can see them for years," says physical therapist DeJong. "A child with developmental delays, such as cerebral palsy, for example, I'll see forever. We get to develop rapport."[47] A physical therapist works with the child and family to set goals for improvement.

Although most therapists work forty-hour weeks, one in four therapists works part-time. Part-time work or consulting is available for those who want a flexible schedule. Ten percent of therapists hold more than one job since the current number of jobs is greater than the number of therapists. A typical workweek may include some weekend and evening shifts, especially for those employed by hospitals. Bartek comments on the various opportunities: "There are so many different areas that you can work in. Our field is very diverse. It gives you a lot of flexibility."[48]

Experience and Leadership to Advance

Physical therapists who wish to move into supervisory positions can do this either by working for several years in their field or through additional education. Experience and leadership qualities prepare therapists to advance to positions in administration. In hospitals, physical therapists may start in a staff position, which is the entry level, and rise to chief physical therapist and then to director of the department. Bartek became the coordinator of rehabilitation services at Texas Sports Medicine Center after five years of experience.

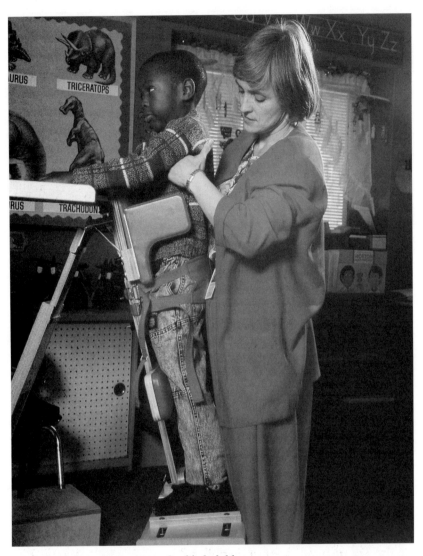

A physical therapist assists a disabled child.

At present, a master's degree is required for advancement to administration, research, or teaching positions. Physical therapists with a master's degree or higher can teach in a college or be involved in research, which adds to information about the effectiveness of prescribed treatments. However, starting in 2002 a master's degree will be the entry-level requirement to become a physical therapist, so it will be only one of many criteria needed for advancement. Job performance and leadership qualities will become more important for promotions.

Some Facts About Physical Therapists

In February 2000 the American Physical Therapy Association listed the following facts about physical therapists on its website (www.apta.org).

- More than two out of three physical therapists are women.
- 78.4 percent of therapists work full-time—only 0.5 percent are retired.
- Although nearly half of all physical therapists work in private outpatient practices or hospitals, 5.5 percent work in schools and less than 1 percent each work in research, wellness facilities, and industries.
- The range of salaries is from less than $30,000 a year (11.5 percent) to over $100,000 a year (4.4 percent), with almost half earning between $45,000 and $70,000 a year.
- Nine out of ten physical therapists are white—about 2 percent are Hispanic and 1.5 percent are black.
- As of 2000, 56 percent of physical therapists held a bachelor's degree, 40.4 percent had a master's degree, and 1.7 percent had a doctorate in physical therapy.

Although all physical therapy programs include training in the care of wounds, it is possible to take additional training in this field and receive certification in wound care from the American Academy of Wound Management. This training is obtained once the basic physical therapy program is completed. Wound care speeds healing for diabetic ulcers, burns, or wounds. Melinda Soto, a physical therapist in Oklahoma, is a certified wound care specialist. Soto says, "There is a great need for quality wound care . . . partly because of our large diabetic population. It is so rewarding to practice in this area of physical therapy because the results of your efforts are so visible. By healing their wound you also enable the person to return to normal activities."[49]

Salaries for Physical Therapists

Salaries for physical therapists vary depending on experience, geographical location, and the therapist's position. In 1998 the median annual earnings for a physical therapist were $56,600, according to the *Occupational Outlook Handbook*. A recent graduate can expect to earn between $40,000 and $45,000 a year.

Therapists with several years' experience have salaries ranging from $54,000 to $81,000 per year, depending on whether they are in a supervisory role. Home health care therapists earned the highest average annual salaries for nonsupervisory positions at $65,000. Hospital-based therapists were at the lower end of the salary range

Over 60 percent of physical therapists are women.

with annual earnings of about $50,000. Self-employed therapists usually earn more than $50,000 a year.

Income for therapists can be increased through opportunities to work extra hours. Those who work evening hours or weekends receive additional money as compensation for working less-desirable shifts.

Physical Therapy in the Twenty-First Century

The field of physical therapy will continue to provide a necessary health care service during the twenty-first century. However, insurance companies are limiting the number of visits that patients can make to a therapist in order to cut costs. This is expected to decrease opportunities for employment in the field until 2003. In the past, a patient might have been allowed six weeks of physical therapy; today, that same patient may be limited to as few as four visits. This has changed the way therapists work. Regarding the current work situation, Bartek says, "We are seeing patients a fewer number of visits. Rather than spending an hour with each patient, we are having to be more efficient. You have to prioritize where the rehab needs to be focused and then you are just seeing more [patients] in a day."[50]

Despite these changes, positions in physical therapy are expected to grow in the years between 2003 and 2008. This growth is due to the current emphasis in society on physical fitness, which leads to sports-related injuries; and the large population of people in their forties and fifties, who are entering the age when diseases that require physical therapy, such as strokes and heart attacks, are more prevalent.

For those interested in a career in health care focusing on rehabilitating sick or injured people, physical therapy is a good field. Physical therapists like working with people on a one-to-one basis and are able to be both positive and encouraging. It is a career offering a lot of personal satisfaction plus a good income.

Chapter 5

Pharmacists

Pharmacists make a unique contribution to the field of health care. Their entire education is based on the science of medications in treating diseases, which makes them the health care workers most knowledgeable in this area. Their expertise extends from the chemical composition of medications to the effects, both good and bad, that medications can produce in a patient. Pharmacists dispense drugs from prescriptions written by physicians and others qualified to prescribe medications.

Because of their education, they are the best source of information for doctors, nurses, and patients who need explanations about drugs. They can explain to the public in easy-to-understand language what a drug does, how to take it, and any negative reactions the drug may have in the human body. The career of a pharmacist is an important one in health care because other health care professionals and the public depend on them to safely fill prescriptions. Failure to do this could result in adverse medication reactions or even the death of a patient.

A Description of the Job

As a specialist in drug therapy, pharmacists dispense medications to patients. They understand what chemicals are in each medication and how those chemicals work in the human body. In the past, many prescriptions required the pharmacist to actually mix chemicals to make drugs. Although occasionally a pharmacist still needs to do this, it is rare since most medications are made by pharmaceutical companies and are delivered to pharmacies ready to dispense. Because of this, many pharmacists feel that their knowledge is underused.

One of the areas in which the mixing of medications is actually done is intravenous fluids, which are infused into a patient's vein via a needle. Pharmacists add drugs, such as antibiotics, to these solutions before delivering them to nurses to administer. In reality, pharmacy technicians, under the supervision of pharmacists, do much of the

71

A pharmacist searches for a patient's medication in a hospital pharmacy.

work of actually counting out pills, preparing solutions, and delivering the medications.

Pharmacists spend most of their day entering prescription data into computers and checking computer programs for information on drugs that have been ordered. In doing this, they look for drugs that are incompatible with medication already prescribed for the patient. They also check for appropriate doses and possible adverse reactions that could occur as a result of taking the medication. Frank Maluda, the owner of an independent pharmacy, says, "The most important role is trying to prevent drug interactions, and the computer helps with that. The software tracks your customer's previous prescriptions and will check for adverse drug reactions."[51]

To fill a drug order, a pharmacist needs a written order from a physician, which is called a prescription. Prescriptions can be delivered to a pharmacy on a prescription pad brought in by a patient or family member or can be received through phone or fax from a doctor, dentist, or other qualified person. In hospitals, the prescriptions come as an order sheet on the patient's chart.

To safely fill prescriptions, the pharmacist must know the patient's diagnosis and any drug allergies. Dispensing medications for children under the age of twelve requires additional safety checks since children vary greatly in weight. A pharmacist must double check a child's dose by calculating the child's weight, determining the drug manufacturer's recommendations, and then checking that the ordered dose is correct. An adult-size dose could be very harmful to a child.

A hospital pharmacist uses his or her knowledge to advise staff physicians and nurses on drugs. Common questions from the nursing staff to the pharmacist concern side effects of medications, proper dosage, how to administer drugs, and whether several drugs being administered to one patient will work together without harmful interactions. Physicians most often ask questions about drugs they

Trends in Pharmacy

The work of a pharmacist has changed greatly over the years. In the past pharmacists mixed chemicals to make medications. Today this is seldom done in a modern pharmacy. Pharmacists used to be the only ones who filled prescriptions; today, however, pharmacy technicians are largely responsible for filling prescriptions. Tim Thornton, a registered pharmacist, says, "Pharmacists are moving from being a dispenser of medications to being a dispenser of knowledge."

The pharmacist today has more time for educating patients, doctors, and nurses because of help from technicians and automation in the pharmacy. Technological equipment is used increasingly in both hospitals and retail pharmacies. This includes the use of computers to store patient and drug information and automated medication dispensing machines, which are stocked by the pharmacy and are used by hospital nurses to obtain patient medications. In the future, doctors will enter their orders for medications directly into a computer linked to a pharmacy. Robots will be used to dispense medication into containers. Despite these changes, there will always be positions for pharmacists and technicians who will need to be available to wait on customers, call physicians, and provide drug knowledge to patients.

need to administer that may be outside their field of expertise. An example of this might be a surgeon whose patient has developed a stomach ulcer, but the surgeon does not usually prescribe medications for this condition. Doctors may also consult the pharmacist about a patient's unusual reaction to a medication.

In retail stores pharmacists counsel patients about any new drug dispensed to them. This counseling includes how to take the drug, when to take it, and unexpected reactions to look for. Some drugs that patients take can have very serious side effects if taken incorrectly. An example is a drug to slow blood-clotting time for patients who have developed clots as part of their illness. Pharmacists explain to the patient to watch for unusual bleeding, like nosebleeds, which could indicate too much medication. Although this drug is monitored by frequent blood tests, it is still important for the patient to know about the dangers of taking it in order to catch early signs of a problem. Because of the potential consequences of inaccurate knowledge being given to a patient, only a registered pharmacist can teach patients about drugs.

A pharmacist counsels a patient about proper use and effects of her medication.

Filling drug orders is one of the main tasks of pharmacists.

Pharmacists are responsible for managing the business side of the pharmacy where they work. They must keep their departments stocked with drugs and equipment and meet with representatives from drug companies. Drug company representatives visit pharmacies to explain the uses and benefits of newly developed medications so that pharmacists will have current information when physicians begin prescribing them.

Retail pharmacists are involved in working with insurance companies that provide coverage for prescription drugs. Many pharmacists are surprised at the amount of time they spend handling insurance claims and filling out records. When speaking of his first year as a pharmacist, Tim Thornton recalls, "I did not realize the business aspect of it would be so critical. I had it in my mind that that was handled by a higher authority in a more centralized location."[52]

Personal Qualifications

Anyone considering a pharmacy career should be the kind of person who pays attention to details. Pharmacists must be willing to check and recheck their work. Mistakes in dispensing medications can cause complications or even death in a patient. While filling prescriptions, it is necessary to concentrate and avoid distractions in order to eliminate potential errors. A clean, ordered work environment also helps reduce errors. Because eliminating mistakes is essential, pharmacists often work on hospital committees charged with identifying why medication errors occur and how to prevent them in the future.

Another part of filling prescriptions safely is the ability to use math to accurately calculate amounts of drugs to use when mixing solutions or when filling prescriptions. If a physician orders a certain strength solution, the pharmacist will need to calculate the amount of medication to add to the solution. There are also times when a pill does not come in the ordered dose and the pharmacist calculates whether more than one pill or even half a pill is required to match the physician's order.

A pharmacist should have high ethical standards. This is necessary because the pharmacist is allowed to handle and dispense habit-forming drugs. Another ethical issue is confidentiality of patient records since pharmacists have information ranging from the patient's age to his or her diagnoses.

To be successful in the profession, pharmacists must be good communicators. Developing a good relationship with patients is as important to a pharmacist as it is to a physician. Thornton, who is a retail pharmacist says, "I feel like I have a good rapport with the older population. I really like talking with them just from the point of being able to make a difference. When they have problems with their medications, I am able to solve that."[53] Good communications with other health care professionals about medication therapy is also necessary.

Educational Requirements Increase

In the past, education for pharmacists took about five years to complete. However, in 2001 pharmacy schools eliminated five-year programs in favor of a six-year curriculum. The move to a six-year curriculum was agreed on in 1992, when a majority of the nation's schools and pharmacy colleges voted in favor of it. The greatest number of pharmacists in the year 2000 held bachelor's degrees from a five-year program. By the year 2005 all accredited pharmacy schools will grant the degree of doctor of pharmacy (Pharm.D), which takes six years to complete. Many pharmacy schools have already graduated their last class of students with a bachelor's degree.

The education of a pharmacist falls into two categories. The first part is two years of prepharmacy courses, followed by four years of pharmacy school, known as professional school. Prepharmacy courses

Law and the Pharmacist

Pharmacists are the most regulated of all medical professions. Every state board of pharmacy has laws that are particular to that state alone, which pharmacists are required to follow. Pharmacists also must adhere to rules from federal agencies such as the Food and Drug Administration and the Drug Enforcement Administration, which controls the use of narcotics and other habit-forming drugs. Medicare and Medicaid, which are federally controlled health plans, have additional rules that a pharmacist must know and practice.

A thorough knowledge of drug laws is necessary to keep the public safe and to prevent misuse and abuse of medications. A pharmacist demonstrates understanding of these laws by passing an examination, which covers the regulations. Licensing examinations for registry as a pharmacist are divided into two parts. The first part of the examination covers laws governing drugs in the state in which the pharmacist plans to practice. If the pharmacist moves to a new state, testing on that state's drug laws is required before a license can be issued. The second part of the examination focuses on knowledge of medications and their use in treating illnesses.

often include mathematics, physics, biology, and chemistry. Some schools of pharmacy require volunteer work in a pharmacy prior to professional school, so the prospective student will have some idea of what the field of pharmacy is about. "Four hundred hours of volunteering is the amount schools are requiring of prospective students,"[54] states Marshall Steglich, the assistant director of the pharmacy at Houston Northwest Medical Center. In addition, some schools expect applicants to take the Pharmacy College Admissions Test. This test can be taken in high school or during the two years of prepharmacy courses. The three-hundred-question multiple choice test covers knowledge of mathematics, science, vocabulary, and reading comprehension.

Once a pharmacy college accepts a student, the curriculum will consist of courses specific to the occupation, such as pharmacology, pharmacy law and ethics, and biochemistry. Pharmacy courses teach students to fill prescriptions, communicate with the public and with health care professionals, and to develop pharmacy management techniques. They also study chemicals used in medications, medications obtained from plants and animals, and the action of drugs in the body.

Before graduation, a student must complete an internship with licensed pharmacists to gain practical experience in the career. This is typically done during the last year of school and involves experiences in retail pharmacies, hospital pharmacies, and by attending patient rounds with physicians in a hospital. In these settings, the intern works just like a registered pharmacist, with the exception that the supervising pharmacist must check all work.

All fifty states require passing the National Association of Boards of Pharmacy Licensing Examination in order to become licensed. Graduation from an approved school and evidence of having served an internship are requirements for a license, which is necessary for employment. Licensed pharmacists can use the designation R.Ph. (registered pharmacist) after their names.

Beyond Retail Stores and Hospitals

After completing professional school, most pharmacists work in retail drugstores, grocery store pharmacies, or in hospitals. Community pharmacies, where patients take prescriptions to be filled, employ about 60 percent of all pharmacists. Hospitals are the second-largest employer of pharmacists. Other areas of employment are Internet pharmacies, home health care agencies, pharmaceutical companies, and the federal government. Government jobs are available in the U.S. Public Health Service, the Department of Veterans Affairs, the armed services, and the Food and Drug Administration. Pharmacists in the Food and Drug Administration work as experts on advisory committees, prepare reports on new drug applications and adverse reactions, and generally work to ensure the safety of drugs. In pharmaceutical companies, pharmacists work as sales representatives and visit physicians' offices to provide information about new drugs on the market. They also research, develop, and market products.

Employment opportunities are anticipated to be the greatest in California, the Southwest, and the Southeast. These are popular retirement areas for older citizens, who often have chronic illnesses that require prescription drugs. Overall, those who work in the profession consider pharmacy a stable profession. Steglich says, "Health care and pharmacy in general have been fairly stable and the demand is generally there. You don't have these peaks and valleys you might have [in other fields] where you get laid off. There is a certain amount of security."[55]

Pharmacists have the option of working part time. Although most pharmacists work forty to forty-four hours a week, one out of seven pharmacists worked part-time in 1998, according to the *Occupational Outlook Handbook*. About twice as many female pharmacists work part-time, compared to their male counterparts. Tim Thornton feels that more women are choosing pharmacy as a career because of the many opportunities to work part-time. Thornton describes the ease of finding part-time work: "I can go to probably any pharmacy in the company [he works for] and say, I just want to pick up a couple of hours."[56] Many pharmacists work a full-time job during the week and then work on their days off at another location to supplement their income. However, opportunities to work

A pharmacist dispenses pills from a sorting machine.

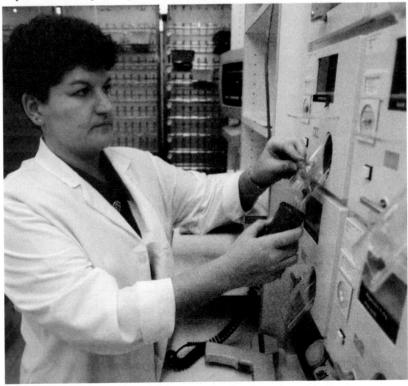

Pharmacy Technicians

Pharmacy technicians work alongside registered pharmacists in both retail and hospital pharmacies. Retail stores employ about 70 percent of all technicians. Technicians do most of the actual counting and dispensing of medications, wait on customers, and call doctors for prescription refills. In hospitals, they prepare intravenous fluids by adding physician-ordered medications to them and fill doctors' orders for oral drugs. Registered pharmacists check all prescriptions filled by technicians. Technicians are not allowed to take new prescription orders over the phone from a physician or to counsel patients about the drugs they are taking.

Most pharmacy technicians have on-the-job training as their educational background, but a few technicians have formal education from a technical school, hospital, or community college. About three-fourths of all professional pharmacy students work as technicians while attending school. Starting in 2001 all pharmacy technicians must pass a certification test after one year of on-the-job training. Technicians who have over ten years of experience will be exempt from the exam.

The pay scale for a technician is not high. In 1998 the average technician was paid about $8.54 an hour.

regular schedules are limited. Most pharmacies, whether in a hospital or in retail, are open seven days a week and must be staffed during evenings and on weekends. In addition, hospitals require twenty-four-hour-a-day staffing since a pharmacist must be on duty at all times.

Professional Advancement

For those who work in hospital or retail pharmacies, the main way to advance is to work up to a supervisory position after years of experience. In retail stores, the pharmacist in charge is referred to as a manager. Retail pharmacists may also advance to administrative positions at the district or regional level. In hospitals, the pharmacist in charge is referred to as the director of the pharmacy. Steglich, an assistant director of a hospital pharmacy, says that opportunities for "upward mobility can be limited in hospitals"[57] since there are just three levels of people working in a pharmacy—pharmacy technicians, staff pharmacists, and a few pharmacists who are in charge.

Some pharmacists choose to own their own pharmacy. In this position, they supervise the entire store. Thornton states, "Probably less than five percent of pharmacists own their own stores, although it is a growing trend."[58] He says that in today's market, where 80 percent of all prescriptions are filled with insurance coverage, small privately owned pharmacies are able to compete with the larger prescription drug companies. However, according to Thornton, "The main thing it takes to own a drugstore is lots of money."[59]

Additional education after graduation from pharmacy school is another way to advance. In a residency, a type of advanced education, a pharmacist specializes in one area of pharmacy. For example, a pharmacist might choose to learn more about pharmacokinetics, which is the study of factors controlling drug absorption in the gastrointestinal tract. Pharmacists with this specialty can obtain positions in which they work more closely with physicians to prescribe better drugs for patients. The pharmacist can advise the physician on the best drug to choose considering a patient's age, disease, and factors affecting drug use by the body.

It is also possible to earn a master of science degree or a doctor of philosophy degree, which will prepare a pharmacist for a job in research. In research, pharmacists study issues like drug compliance in tuberculosis, medication errors, or the correctness of Internet drug information. These studies can be individually conducted with a research grant or can result from surveys retail pharmacists fill out for drug companies.

Salaries for Pharmacists

Salaries for pharmacists are among the highest for any health care professional, which makes the career attractive to many. In 1998, the median annual earnings for all types of pharmacists were $66,220, according to the *Occupational Outlook Handbook*. Pharmacists who work for pharmaceutical companies can earn as much as $81,000 a year. According to the Bureau of Labor Statistics, drug manufacturers typically pay their employees more than other manufacturers. Pharmacist Steglich comments, "Compensation is a plus in terms of what pharmacists are paid. If you eliminate hospital administration and physicians, pharmacists have probably the highest paid positions."[60]

Average starting salaries for pharmacists can range from $49,500 to $61,000 a year. Managers of retail pharmacies or directors of hospital pharmacies earn additional money due to their increased responsibilities. Wage Web, which surveys salary data for many jobs, indicates that the average salary for a pharmacy director, in June 2000, was $68,083, with the maximum average salary reported at

Pharmacists confer on an insurance claim.

$74,144. Health maintenance organizations (HMOs) average $73,000 a year for their pharmacists, which is more than supermarkets, hospitals, or chain drug stores pay.

Salaries are determined by the location and size of the employer's business. Salaries have been highest on the West Coast, where the cost of living is more expensive, and lowest in the South. Large pharmacies pay more than small ones. Many pharmacists have the opportunity for bonuses, which can increase their total pay.

Pharmacists in the Twenty-First Century

Since pharmacists provide a vital service to the community and to other health care professionals, their services are in demand. Factors that indicate a good job market in the future for pharmacists are the increase in number of elderly people in the United States and in the number of prescriptions being written. Older people generally have illnesses that require more medications than younger people take. Between 1992 and 1999, the number of retail prescriptions increased 44 percent in the United States.

The current shortage of pharmacists also makes the job outlook good. The six-year length of the new curriculum has been a deterrent for some considering the career. Another factor in the current shortage is that pharmacists are leaving the profession, especially in retail, because of working longer hours with less help. Retail and research will offer many positions, but hospital positions will not increase as rapidly due to more patients being treated at home. Pharmacists who are educated in the cost versus the benefits of drugs, which compares the effects of similar drugs used to treat an illness to determine if less-expensive drugs work as well as more expensive ones, will also find jobs plentiful in the future.

Chapter 6

Emergency Medical Technicians

Over 14 million calls are made every year in the United States asking for emergency medical help. Emergency medical technicians (EMTs) treat patients during medical emergencies, before they see a physician. EMTs are often the first professional at the scene of an accident and are able to provide help in critical situations, often saving lives in the process. Greg Kunkel, an emergency medical service chief in Houston, says, "It is a wonderful job because you get immediate gratification. The patient improves and you see that. You get immediate feedback and gratitude from the patient."[61]

Emergency medical technician is one of the newest professions in the health care field. The profession began in Europe during the mid-1960s, when it was discovered that private citizens who received treatment for heart attacks prior to being transported by ambulances to hospitals had a much higher rate of survival. Before that time, ambulances were mainly transportation vehicles, with the driver being the only person aboard other than the patient. No emergency care was provided at the scene or during transport. During the last quarter of the twentieth century, the profession changed from being staffed mainly by volunteers, such as nurses, former military medics or corpsmen, or people trained in first aid, to being a profession in which formal education in lifesaving techniques is required, along with certification in the field.

Responding to an Emergency

Emergency medical technicians respond to many kinds of emergencies, such as automobile accidents, heart attacks, drownings, and gunshot wounds. An Amtrak train derailment in Kansas in 2000 required the services of ten ambulances and twenty-eight paramedics and EMTs. The EMTs treated and transported thirty-two people to local hospitals. Cynthia Wentworth, a director of American Medical Response, says, "Injuries ranged from an internal spleen injury to minor abrasions and contusions. These patients were very fortunate and, thankfully, there were no fatalities in this incident."[62]

When an accident or medical emergency happens, the call for help usually comes to EMTs through a 911 operator. When responding to calls, Woodrow Poitier, a paramedic, says, "My main duty is to preserve life and limb. Whenever we're called for an emergency, we

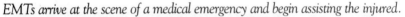

EMTs arrive at the scene of a medical emergency and begin assisting the injured.

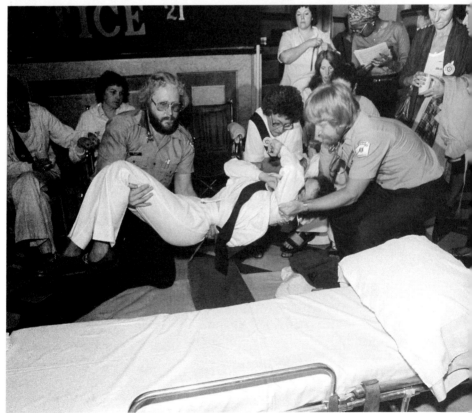

go out and try to take care of the problem. Every call is different."[63] Most EMTs work out of ambulances, which are placed in strategic spots around their service area to shorten the travel time to an emergency. Ambulances are staffed with two EMTs, one of whom drives the ambulance, while the other monitors the patient's condition and provides care.

EMTs follow strict guidelines in various medical situations. Many of the emergencies they respond to can be handled by following general rules. In more complicated cases, a medical doctor, who is usually located at the hospital where they plan to transport the patient, can send instructions via radio.

After arriving at the site of the emergency, EMTs assess the nature and extent of an injury or illness to determine what care needs to be given to a victim. They check the ABCs of emergency care—airway, breathing, and circulation. Their assessments include asking themselves the following questions: Does the patient have an open airway? Is the patient breathing? Is there circulation, determined by a pulse, which means the heart is beating? If there is an absence of any of these, the EMT performs cardiopulmonary resuscitation (CPR) to restore heartbeat and breathing. The EMT performs CPR by supplying air to the patient with an Ambu-bag—which is a face mask attached to an air chamber that can be squeezed to force oxygen into a patient's lungs—and by performing chest compressions to restore a heartbeat.

Once CPR is successfully accomplished, the EMT takes care of injuries such as bleeding, fractures, and burns. When the immediate emergency is resolved and the patient's condition has stabilized, an ambulance transfers the patient to the nearest hospital to receive further care by a physician. Once at the hospital emergency department, the EMTs move the patient inside, report to the doctors and nurses what assistance has been given, and may continue to assist, depending on the situation. EMTs respond to many emergencies during a typical day. Stacey Moore, a paramedic in Houston, says, "The best thing about being a paramedic for an EMS [emergency medical service] is that when you come to work you never know what will happen."[64]

Remaining Calm in Emergencies

The most important quality for an EMT to possess is the ability to make good decisions in stressful situations. "It takes a certain type of

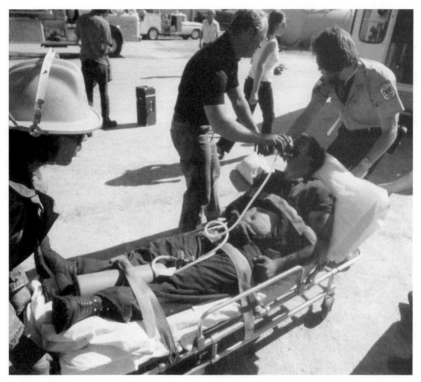

After resolving the immediate emergency, EMTs transfer a patient to the nearest hospital for further treatment.

person for this job. You have to love working under stress and in a crisis situation,"[65] comments Greg Kunkel. Since every situation involves an emergency, EMTs must remain calm while quickly devising a plan of action. EMTs are trained to perform a thorough but speedy assessment of the situation and then to care for the most life-threatening symptoms first. Life-or-death situations are always high stress, and bystanders, whose emotions often get out of control, can add to this, making it important for an EMT to focus on the patient alone while making decisions about needed care.

Despite the high stress level accompanying the position, the job attracts people who like excitement, challenges, and the opportunity to help people. Melissa Gorman, who worked as an EMT while a student at the University of California, Los Angeles, says, "I realized that I needed to work in a fast paced environment where I was constantly being challenged."[66] A job as an EMT offers immense rewards related to the satisfaction of saving lives and helping those who are in life-threatening situations.

Good judgment is also a necessary requirement for EMTs. Many of their decisions about care are based on what they see or hear without the advantage of sophisticated laboratory tests or X rays. EMTs need to recognize when something is wrong or about to go wrong, so they can take appropriate action. They must quickly use logic to come to a conclusion and decide if the conclusion makes sense in that particular situation. For example, when responding to an unconscious patient, an EMT needs to determine if the patient fainted, was a diabetic with low blood sugar, or perhaps had some other medical condition, like hypotensive (low blood pressure) shock, that needs treatment. Each of these conditions would be handled differently.

The job also requires physical stamina. Getting to an accident scene outdoors may require climbing, stooping, crawling, or even wading through water. The actual care of a patient at an accident scene usually requires the EMT to kneel while administering treatment. EMTs may be involved in helping free victims trapped in automobiles, cave-ins of ditches, or the collapse of a building. One of the stated requirements by some departments who hire EMTs is that they must be able to lift one hundred pounds or, at the least, be able to lift and carry heavy loads.

EMTs also need good communication skills. EMTs must be good listeners as well as good at knowing appropriate questions to ask. At an accident scene or a home where they have been called, they will need to communicate with the patient or family to get information about what led to the event and to obtain information, if possible, about the patient's medical background that might influence care. "You have to learn how to interact with people at their worst," says Gary Bennett, a firefighter and EMT intermediate. "Sometimes you don't take them [patients] to the hospital. You provide what care they need on the spot and just give emotional assistance. Some people just want to hear a caring voice."[67] EMTs often communicate by radio with a physician at a hospital emergency department to get additional instructions for care; thus, their ability to do clear, concise reporting of events is vital for the physician who makes decisions before even seeing the patient.

Levels of EMT Care

There are four levels of providers of emergency medical service (EMS): first responders, EMT basic, EMT intermediate, and EMT

Helicopter Paramedics

An exciting possibility for paramedics is a position with a hospital helicopter emergency transport team. Most major U.S. cities have at least one hospital or government group that uses helicopters to transport trauma victims. These air ambulance services frequently have names such as Life Flight or Medflight attached to the name of the hospital or city providing the service.

A typical crew on a Life Flight helicopter consists of a pilot; a flight nurse, who is both a registered nurse and a certified paramedic; and a flight paramedic. Each crew member is highly qualified, with numerous certifications and several years' prior ambulance, critical care, or emergency room experience.

The purpose of helicopter ambulances is to transport critically ill or injured persons as rapidly as possible to a hospital where the emergency department and its personnel are especially equipped to handle major trauma cases. During flight, the nurse and paramedic work together to provide advanced lifesaving procedures. Fifty to 60 percent of the flights made are to motor vehicle accidents, with a smaller percentage being gunshot wounds, falls, burns, and industrial accidents. The helicopter flies within the city as well as to surrounding counties, with a range of about 150 miles.

Helicopters allow paramedics to rescue trauma victims quickly and efficiently.

paramedic. Each level requires more education than the previous one and equips the person for increasing responsibility when providing care.

First responders are the lowest level of emergency help. In some states, people in this position are called emergency care attendants. They are not called EMTs, but they are part of the emergency response system. The name *first responder* is given because they are more likely to arrive at accidents or fires before EMTs and are often firefighters or police officers. They make the decision as to whether more advanced emergency care is needed while administering first aid.

EMT basic is the first level of provider who is called an emergency medical technician. These EMTs are taught to assess a patient to determine the severity of the accident or medical emergency.

Paramedics attend a child who injured herself bicycling.

Their training enables them to control bleeding, administer oxygen, and restore breathing. Other skills learned include how to immobilize fractures, bandage wounds, assist heart attack victims, and give initial care in a variety of situations. This level of technician is also known as EMT 1.

The intermediate level of emergency medical technician is called an EMT 2 (or sometimes an EMT 3). Their training is more advanced than the two previous levels. In addition to the skills of the first responders and the EMT basics, an EMT 2 knows how to administer intravenous fluids, manage shock in cardiac arrest, and insert endotracheal tubes (from the mouth to the trachea) to assist with breathing.

The highest level of emergency care in the field is provided by an EMT 4, also called a paramedic. At this level, the EMT can administer medications both by mouth or by IV; interpret EKGs, which are tracings of the electrical activity of the heart; and use equipment to monitor various internal functions.

Equipment used by all EMTs in the performance of their jobs includes use of backboards to immobilize back injuries, stretchers to move patients about, splints for care of sprains or fractures, and oxygen equipment for breathing problems, in addition to previously mentioned items.

Educational Requirements

The education of an EMT depends on the level of training a person wishes to acquire. Training to become an emergency medical technician can be obtained at police, fire, and health departments; hospitals; and in colleges or universities as a degree or nondegree course. Many schools offer an associate of applied science degree in a two-year course for paramedics.

Positions as an EMT can be obtained with less time spent in formal education than most other health care jobs. One hundred hours to two years of training can prepare a person for a position in emergency care. Gary Bennett considers the tiered educational levels to become an EMT an advantage: "You don't have to dive off into a two-year or four-year educational program without knowing what you are getting into—[by starting at the lower levels of care] you get a taste of what it is like to actually get hands-on in a health career."[68]

All candidates for EMT programs must be at least eighteen years old and have a high school diploma and a driver's license since

EMTs also drive the ambulances. Paramedic training usually requires the applicant to be at least twenty-one years old because it takes that long to advance through the lower levels and earn the necessary experience.

A basic educational course of 100 to 120 hours of instruction is part of the education for all EMTs. First aid and emergency skills are taught and are combined with time in an emergency room or an ambulance. This initial course will qualify the EMT as an EMT basic provider of care.

Becoming an EMT 2 or 3 (intermediate) adds additional hours of instruction to the basic educational courses. One-year courses at a community college can include time in the emergency room, ambulance, labor and delivery, and the operating room. A technician at this level also learns to use advanced airway devices, such as endotracheal tubes, and to administer intravenous fluids.

To become a paramedic (EMT 4), the technician needs to complete an additional 750 to 1,000 plus hours of coursework, depending on requirements in the state offering the program. Since each state sets up requirements for certification, they can also dictate the length of programs. An example of some of the classes offered are medical terminology, infection control, how to perform a physical examination, and medication knowledge and administration. In learning to perform a physical examination on a patient, a paramedic learns to differentiate sounds heard in the lungs and heart and to perform tests to determine neurological functioning (functioning of the brain and spinal cord). Medication knowledge concentrates heavily on the use of emergency drugs, such as those needed for cardiac arrests. Internships with additional emergency care experience are part of the training.

All fifty states and the District of Columbia require EMTs to pass a certification examination in order to work. State certification is obtained by taking an examination administered by the state in which the EMT is employed. Thirty-nine states require registration of EMTs through the National Registry of Emergency Medical Technicians (NREMT). The NREMT registers EMS employees at all four levels. To be registered, the person must pass written and performance examinations. NREMT registration is an additional acknowledgment of an EMT's qualifications and may enhance chances for jobs with higher salaries.

Water Rescue Training for Paramedics

Paramedics working in areas where there are a lot of water sports or large bodies of water are sometimes trained in water rescues. In many parts of the country, trained divers must rescue underwater victims before EMTs can give emergency care. Underwater rescue training allows EMTs to immediately begin caring for victims—if they are the first on the scene—so that the accident victims receive care without delay.

The paramedics use this training to assist swimmers in distress, help jet ski accident victims, search underwater for people who have fallen into the water or who are submerged underwater in cars, and to treat people with neck or spine injuries who have been in diving accidents. Equipment used includes diving masks, swim fins, snorkels, gloves, rope, rescue tubes, and devices to cut the seat belts of people trapped underwater in automobiles.

EMTs must reregister every two years to maintain certification. Further requirements for recertification include current employment as an EMT and proof of continuing education. To stay current, an EMT periodically takes courses such as prevention of exposure to AIDS or the treatment of chest injuries.

Job Opportunities

Job opportunities for emergency medical technicians vary according to location. Most EMTs work in or near large cities because opportunities for paid positions are greater there. Rural emergency services are frequently staffed with volunteers, making paid jobs scarcer in those areas. Statistics in 1995 indicated that a little over half of all EMTs were part-time volunteers.

Approximately 30 percent of EMTs work for fire, police, or rescue squads. Positions in fire or police departments are the most desirable because of higher pay and more benefits. There is more competition for these jobs, and those applying to be paramedics with these agencies are usually trained to be firefighters and police officers as well as EMTs.

An EMT awaits the next emergency call.

Different groups operate emergency medical services depending on the part of the country. In addition to fire and police departments, which hire EMTs, other employers of EMTs are hospitals, which hire 20 percent of them, and ambulance services, which employ about 50 percent. Another employment opportunity is with private ambulance companies, which employ EMTs to accompany patients during nonemergency situations when they are being transferred between care facilities.

There is a high job turnover rate due to the stress of the profession. Statistics indicate that the average EMT stays in the profession only about eight years. Those paramedics who work for police or fire departments are often cross-trained as firefighters or police officers to allow them occasional time away from the daily stress of dealing with medical emergencies.

Disadvantages

Although emergency work can be an exciting career, the constant exposure to stressful situations can lead to burnout. Jim Beach, a paramedic in Los Angeles since 1987, comments about how stress has affected his family life: "I used to have a problem . . . taking my day's work home with me. I was trying to run my family like I would at the fire station."[69] Beach explains that he went to counseling to learn how to separate the stresses of his job from his home life.

Defibrillators

A defibrillator is a piece of equipment used by EMTs during the emergency care of patients. Defibrillation is used for patients whose hearts are malfunctioning because the heart's electrical current no longer causes it to beat effectively. This cardiac arrest is not always caused by a heart attack; abnormal rhythms of the heart are also responsible.

An automatic external defibrillator (AED) is used by EMTs when they respond to a cardiac emergency. An AED is about the size of a laptop computer and contains an electrical current. To use a defibrillator, an EMT places electrodes on the patient's chest and pushes a button to deliver a pulse of electricity to restart the heart in a normal rhythm. If the original shock does not convert the abnormal rhythm, multiple shocks can be given.

The newest defibrillators are so advanced that people with no medical training can be taught to use them. In 1999 a group of sixth-graders was taught how to use automatic external defibrillators and then performed the procedure nearly as well as EMTs who were also learning for the first time. The defibrillator has a built-in computer, which can detect a patient's abnormal heart rhythm. This is important since not all abnormal rhythms can be corrected with this machine. The machine is 90 percent accurate in detecting correctable rhythms. The AED gives verbal or visual cues, telling the operator when to push the button to deliver the electric current. If the problem cannot be corrected with an electric shock, the AED will not deliver the current. AEDs are not used on children under the age of eight or children weighing less than fifty-five pounds.

Another disadvantage is the working conditions. Although some EMTs work inside hospital emergency departments, many are employed by ambulance services, which require outdoor work in all types of weather, including rain and snow. EMTs are expected to lift and move patients on and off stretchers, which introduces the possibility of back injury if proper body mechanics are not used. Frequent exposure to the high decibels of ambulance sirens can, over time, damage hearing. According to a federal study done in 1986, ambulance drivers are exposed to higher-than-recommended levels of sound. Four additional studies have linked hearing loss to the noise of sirens.

EMTs also face exposure to infectious diseases, particularly those involving blood, such as hepatitis B and AIDS. However, there is a vaccine for hepatitis B, which is required for those working as EMTs. There is also the possibility of exposure to airborne infections, such as tuberculosis or influenza, in the close confines of an ambulance. Like other health care professionals, EMTs are taught ways to minimize exposure by using masks, wearing gloves and gowns, and by washing hands.

In addition, the work schedule of EMTs involves long hours, alternating between days and evenings, and requires holiday and weekend work. Emergency services must be staffed twenty-four hours a day, seven days a week, every day of the year. Some EMTs are on call for twenty-four to forty-eight hours at a time. Gary Bennett's work schedule for a fire department requires him to work twenty-four hours on duty, followed by forty-eight hours off duty, which he says is a pretty common schedule. The average workweek for EMTs can range from forty-five to sixty hours a week, which is longer than most health professionals, with the exception of physicians.

Limited Advancement Opportunities

Opportunities to advance within the levels of EMTs are limited, except for lower levels of EMTs who want to advance from EMT basic to EMT intermediate and then to EMT paramedic. Opportunities beyond EMT paramedic include supervisor, clinical manager, and operations manager. However, supervisory positions usually mean giving up direct emergency care.

Supervisors guide the work of all EMS crews on a shift, including setting priorities for ambulance response, dispatching the crews, and handling paperwork. Harry Small, an EMS commander, oversees supervisors and sixty-five paramedics at a large city fire department. His job covers everything from setting up EMT training and ordering supplies to planning a department budget. "I used to be out there as a paramedic, but now my job is to make sure that all the EMTs and paramedics have everything they need to do their job."[70] With additional education and experience, it is possible to become an EMT instructor. Other positions, which are related, but outside the field, are dispatcher and sales and marketing of emergency medical equipment.

Some EMTs use their education as a stepping-stone to return to school to become registered nurses, physicians, or physician assistants. Since EMTs average only eight years in the profession, acquiring more education allows them to remain in health care in a related field in which the stress level is less intense, the pay scale is higher, and the benefits are more readily available. EMTs can receive as much as two semesters' credit toward a nursing degree in some schools.

Salaries for EMTs

The amount of money an EMT earns is related to the place of employment, the amount of training, and the number of years of experience. Paramedics, because of their greater training and responsibility, earn more than EMT basic or intermediate emergency care workers. The average starting salary for all types of EMTs in 1997 was $20,000. Those with experience averaged $31,000. Overall, salaries for EMTs tend to be lower than salaries for others who work in health care. Two factors relate to the lower salaries. One factor is the number of volunteers who still staff emergency medical services. The other factor relates to an EMT's formal education, which is less than most other health care fields require.

Fire departments and police departments who employ EMTs pay the highest salaries. In addition, EMTs who work for fire or police departments receive paid vacations and holidays, health insurance, and retirement plans. The average salary in 1997 for EMTs or paramedics in fire departments was about $35,000 a year. Large city fire departments often pay EMTs more. A 1999 article in the Los Angeles Business Journal stated that paramedics working for the Los Angeles Fire Department can earn an average of $65,000 a year and up to $100,000, if they are willing to work extra hours. For example, Jim Beach says he has worked as many as "170 hours of overtime a month."[71]

Some cities pay more for EMTs who have graduated from a community college EMS program. Houston pays EMTs with community college degrees starting salaries in the mid to upper $20,000s, with advancement to $50,000 after ten years. Paramedic positions start at $28,000. Many paramedics increase their earning potential by becoming shift supervisors, a position paying as much as $43,100 a year.

Private ambulance companies and hospitals typically pay less than government agencies, such as fire departments. These positions

Paramedics stabilize an injured child.

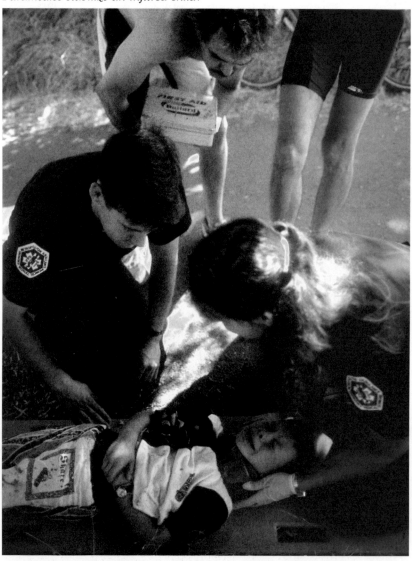

frequently do not offer benefits like retirement plans. The 1997 average salary paid by private ambulance firms to EMTs was $18,300 per year, and hospitals paid EMTs $19,900 a year.

Emergency Medical Technicians in the Twenty-First Century

The twenty-first century is predicted to be a time of job growth for EMTs. The *Occupational Outlook Handbook* predicts that EMTs will have a faster-than-average job growth through 2008. Hospitals and private ambulance services will provide the most new jobs. New York State is predicting it will need 254 more emergency medical technicians a year through 2007. The aging population in the United States is a factor in the growth of the profession. Also, more emergency care positions are changing from volunteer to paid, which opens new positions every day for salaried EMTs. The high turnover rate in the field, due to stress and limited advancement opportunities, also creates new openings on an ongoing basis. In the few years since positions as EMTs have evolved, the profession has added greatly to the health of our nation by providing a vital new service for those in life-or-death situations.

Notes

Introduction: Combining Science and Service

1. Tim Thornton, interview by author, The Woodlands, TX, March 11, 2001.

2. Quoted in Shirley H. Fondiller and Barbara J. Nerone, *Nursing: The Career of a Lifetime.* New York: National League of Nursing, 1995, p.16.

3. Kenneth Callen, letter to author, March 12, 2001.

4. Gary Bennett, interview by author, The Woodlands, TX, April 25, 2001.

5. Kelly Bartek, interview by author, Tomball, TX, April 3, 2001.

Chapter 1: Nurses

6. Quoted in Andrew Morkes, ed., *What Can I Do Now? Preparing for a Career in Nursing.* Chicago: Ferguson, 1998, p. 81.

7. Rosemary Luquire, "All Hospitals Can Do the Same to Attract Nurses," *Houston Chronicle,* August 27, 2001, p. 21A.

8. Sandy Cacciatore, interview by author, Tomball, TX, January 19, 2001.

9. Quoted in Fondiller and Nerone, *Nursing,* p. 17.

10. Cacciatore, interview.

11. Cacciatore, interview.

12. Cacciatore, interview.

13. Cacciatore, interview.

14. Cacciatore, interview.

15. Quoted in Blythe Camenson, *Real People Working in Health Care.* Lincolnwood, IL: VGM Career Horizons, 1997, p. 31.

16. Quoted in Barbara Finkelstein, ed., *My First Year as a Nurse.* New York: Signet, 1997, p. 88.

17. Quoted in Camenson, *Real People Working in Health Care,* p. 3.

Chapter 2: Physicians

18. Quoted in Melissa Ramsdell, ed., *My First Year as a Doctor*. New York: Walker, 1994, p. 9.

19. Quoted in Ramsdell, *My First Year as a Doctor*, p. 76.

20. Quoted in Ramsdell, *My First Year as a Doctor*, p. 10.

21. Quoted in Camenson, *Real People Working in Health Care*, p. 3.

22. Quoted in Camenson, *Real People Working in Health Care*, p. 4.

23. Quoted in Camenson, *Real People Working in Health Care*, p. 6.

24. Howard Scott, letter to author, March 12, 2001.

25. Quoted in Ramsdell, *My First Year as a Doctor*, p. 17.

26. Quoted in Ramsdell, *My First Year as a Doctor*, p.81.

27. Callen, letter.

28. Quoted in Ramsdell, *My First Year as a Doctor*, pp. vii and viii.

29. Scott, letter.

Chapter 3: Medical Technologists

30. Joyce McCalmon Jones, letter to author, March 27, 2001.

31. Quoted in Holli R. Cosgrove, ed., *Exploring Technical Careers*, vol. 2. Chicago: Ferguson, 1995, p. 492.

32. Quoted in *Kiwi Careers*, "Personal Profile: Nalita Bali," February 8, 2001. www.careers.co.nz/jobs/3e_hte/j80133f.htm.

33. Jones, letter.

34. Jones, letter.

35. Jones, letter.

36. Jones, letter.

37. Jones, letter.

38. Jones, letter.

39. Quoted in Megan Malugani, "Job Q and A," Monster Healthcare, September 7, 2000. www.medsearch.com/qanda/jones.

40. Quoted in Amy Fletcher, "Workers for Med Labs in Short Supply," *Denver Business Journal*, July 13, 2001.http://denver.bcentral.com/denver/stories/2001/07/16/story4.html.

Chapter 4: Physical Therapists

41. Quoted in Camenson, *Real People Working in Health Care*, p. 86.
42. Quoted in Camenson, *Real People Working in Health Care*, p. 87.
43. Bartek, interview.
44. Bartek, interview.
45. Quoted in K. Pica Kahn, "Therapists Work Hard to Keep Energized and Educated About Their Patients' Therapy Needs," *Health Care Professional Update*, vol. 8, no. 4, *Houston Chronicle Supplement*, April 2001, p. 7.
46. Bartek, interview.
47. Quoted in Camenson, *Real People Working in Health Care*, p. 86.
48. Bartek, interview.
49. Quoted in *Ponca City News*, "SJRMC Physical Therapy Provides Wound Care Plan," October 17, 1999. www.poncacitynews.com/NewsArchives/1099folder/10101799.html.
50. Bartek, interview.

Chapter 5: Pharmacists

51. Quoted in Camenson, *Real People Working in Health Care*, p. 119.
52. Thornton, interview.
53. Thornton, interview.
54. Marshall Steglich, interview by author, Houston, TX, March 9, 2001.
55. Steglich, interview.
56. Thornton, interview.
57. Steglich, interview.
58. Thornton, interview.
59. Thornton, interview.
60. Steglich, interview.

Chapter 6: Emergency Medical Technicians

61. Quoted in K. Pica Kahn, "Being a Paramedic Takes a Special Type of Person," *Health Care Professional Update*, vol. 8, no. 5, *Houston Chronicle Supplement*, May 2001, p. 3.

62. Quoted in *Business Wire*, "Response to Amtrak Derailment in Kansas," March 15, 2000. www.findarticles.com/cf_0/m OEIN/2000_March_15/6010070.../article.jhtml?term=EMT.

63. Quoted in Camenson, *Real People Working in Health Care*, p. 46.

64. Quoted in Kahn, "Being a Paramedic Takes a Special Type of Person," p. 3.

65. Quoted in Kahn, "Being a Paramedic Takes a Special Kind of Person," p. 3.

66. Quoted in University of California, Los Angeles, "EMS Alumni." www.ucpd.ucla.edu/ucpd/ems/alumni.htm.

67. Gary Bennett, interview by author, The Woodlands, TX, April 25, 2001.

68. Bennett, interview.

69. Quoted in Deborah Belgum, "Stress, Horror of Job Mean a High Level of Burnouts," *Los Angeles Business Journal*, November 8, 1999, p. 2. www.findarticles.com/m5072/45_21/57824434/p1/article.jhtml.

70. Quoted in Camenson, *Real People Working in Health Care*, p. 48.

71. Quoted in Belgum, "Stress, Horror of Job Means a High Level of Burnouts," p. 2.

Organizations to Contact

Nurses

American Association of Colleges of Nursing (AACN)
1 Dupont Circle NW, Suite 530
Washington, DC 20036
(202) 463-6930
website: www.aacn.nche.edu

The AACN serves as a national voice for baccalaureate and higher-degree nursing education programs. They work for quality education standards.

American Nurses Association (ANA)
600 Maryland Ave. SW
Washington, DC 20024
(800) 274-4262
website: www.nursingworld.org

This is the primary professional organization for registered nurses in the United States. They lobby government on health care concerns and promote economic and welfare issues for nurses in the workplace.

National Association for Practical Nurse
Education and Service, Inc.
1400 Spring St., Suite 330
Silver Spring, MD 20910
(301) 588-2941
email: napnes@bellatlantic.net

NAPNES promotes high quality education for practical nurses and provides public information about LPNs.

National League for Nursing (NLN)
61 Broadway
New York, NY 10006
(800) 669-1656
website: www.nln.org

This was the first nursing organization in the United States. Their goal is to advance quality nursing education.

Physicians

American Association of Colleges of Osteopathic Medicine (AACOM)
5550 Friendship Blvd., Suite 310
Chevy Chase, MD 20815-7321
(301) 968-4100
website: www.aacom.org

They support and assist osteopathic medical schools. They have a centralized application process to schools in their membership and promote research and government relations related to health care.

American Medical Association (AMA)
Department of Communications and Public Relations
515 N. State St.
Chicago, IL 60610
(312) 464-5000
website: www.ama-assn.org

The AMA is the primary professional organization for medical doctors. Their stated purpose is to promote professionalism in medicine and set standards for medical education, practice, and ethics. They also provide information to the public.

American Osteopathic Association (AOA)
Department of Public Relations
142 E. Ontario St.
Chicago, IL 60611
(800) 621-1773
website: www.aoa-net.org

They provide information on schools, jobs, and statistics regarding their profession.

Association of American Medical Colleges (AAMC)
Section for Student Services
2450 N St. NW
Washington, DC 20037-1131

(202) 828-0400
website: www.aamc.org

This is an association representing medical schools, professional societies, teaching hospitals, and health systems. They work to improve education, advance research in health services, and to integrate education into health care.

Medical Technologists

American Medical Technologists (AMT)
710 Higgins Rd.
Park Ridge, IL 60068
(847) 823-5169
website: www.amt1.com

Certification of technologists in a variety of lab-related professions is offered through the organization. They also provide continuing education credits, have annual conventions, and serve as a professional organization.

American Society of Clinical Pathologists (ASCP)
Board of Registry
PO Box 12277
Chicago, IL 60612
(312) 738-1336
website: www.ascp.org/bor

The ASCP certifies workers in the field of laboratory medicine. Their website provides information on laboratory careers and where to locate accredited programs.

Physical Therapists

American Physical Therapy Association (APTA)
1111 N. Fairfax St.
Alexandria, VA 22314-1488
(800) 999-2782
website: www.apta.org

The APTA is a national professional organization representing physical therapists. Its goal is advancing physical therapy practice, research, and education.

Pharmacists

American Association of Colleges of Pharmacy (AACP)
1426 Prince St.
Alexandria, VA 22314
(703) 739-2330
website: www.aacp.org

This is the national organization representing the interests of pharmaceutical education by working for excellence in the education of students.

American Society of Health-System Pharmacists (ASHP)
7272 Wisconsin Ave.
Bethesda, MD 20814
(301) 657-3000
website: www.ashp.org

They support the professional practice of pharmacy and represent members on issues related to medication use and public health.

Emergency Medical Technicians

National Association of Emergency Medical Technicians (NAEMT)
408 Monroe St.
Clinton, MS 39056
(800) 346-2368
website: www.naemt.org

The NAEMT represents the views and opinions of EMTs. They provide educational programs and work on developing national standards for care provided by EMTs.

National Registry of Emergency Medical Technicians (NREMT)
PO Box 29233
Columbus, OH 43229
(614) 888-4484
website: www.nremt.org

This organization registers EMS providers in the United States.

For Further Reading

Books

David Dorling, *Beyond 2000—the Health Revolution, Surgery, and Medicine in the Twenty-First Century*. Parsippany, NJ: Dillon, 1996. For those interested in some of the newer technology being used in treating patients, this is an interesting book. A few of the new pieces of equipment described are robo-surgeons, computerized artificial body parts, PET scans, and new hearing and vision technology.

Florence Downs and Dorothy Brooten, *New Careers in Nursing*. New York: Arco, 1984. This is a comprehensive look at some of the many available jobs in the field of nursing. Jobs in nursing education, community health, government nursing, and extended care are explored. The book serves as a resource on nursing education.

Leonard Everett Fisher, *The Doctors*. New York: Benchmark Books, 1997. A historical look at doctors in colonial times and doctors who were instrumental in the founding of America is the emphasis of this book. Seventeenth- and eighteenth-century medicine, including Indian remedies and medicinal herbs, is also discussed.

Cheryl Hancock, with Lauren Starkey, *EMT Career Starter*. 2nd ed. New York: Learning Express, 1998. For people looking into a career as an EMT, this is a good book. It describes the steps to becoming an EMT, along with two appendices with information.

Robert James, *Physical Therapists*. Rourke, 1995. The book is aimed at younger readers and describes what physical therapists do and their educational process.

Alex Kacen, *Opportunities in Paramedical Careers*. Lincolnwood, IL: VGM Career Horizons, 1985. Several health care careers are described, including physician assistant, nurse practitioner, medical assistant, emergency medical technician, and physical therapy assistant. There are seven appendices describing programs.

More Brainpower, "Careers and Professions." www.spartacus.school net.co.uk/Wcareer.htm. Several pages of this article discuss the history of women in medicine in England. Specifically designed for students.

Anne Mountfield, *Looking Back at Medicine*. Needham, MA: Schoolhouse, 1988. Famous doctors and nurses, the first hospital, and early disease knowledge are covered in this book. A look at medicine of the future is included.

Ceel Pastenak, *Cool Careers for Girls in Health*. Manassas Park, VA: Impact, 1999. The careers of doctors, dentists, nutritionists, and others are included. The book is written with preteens in mind.

Terence Sacks, *Careers in Medicine*. Lincolnwood, IL: VGM Career Horizons, 1993. A variety of information aimed at becoming a physician is offered. Knowledge is included on how to get into medical school and how to finance a medical school education. The history of medicine and a look at the future gives an overall view of the field.

Websites

American Assembly for Men in Nursing (http://aamn.free yellow.com). This site contains basic information about this organization for men in nursing.

Continuing Education.com., "Continuing Education for EMT." (www.continuingeducation.com/emt). This website lists online courses for EMT continuing education with the prices and the number of credit hours.

Medical-Legal Consulting Institute, Inc. (www.legalnurse.com). Information on how to become a legal nurse consultant is given, along with salary ranges per hour for services.

Works Consulted

Books

Blythe Camenson, *Real People Working in Health Care*. Lincolnwood, IL: VGM Career Horizons, 1997. Thirteen health care careers are examined, including veterinary medicine, dentistry, speech pathology, and dietary science. Each chapter contains one to three interviews with professionals in that field.

Holli R. Cosgrove, ed., *Encyclopedia of Careers and Vocational Guidance*. Vol. 4. 11th ed. Chicago: Ferguson, 2000. A reference book of jobs, giving the history of each profession along with information about the career.

———, *Exploring Technical Careers*. Vol. 2. Chicago: Ferguson, 1995. A book about careers that require technical education but not necessarily a college degree.

Thelma Daley, Norman Feingold, and Bill Katz, eds., *Career Information Center*. Vol. 7. 7th ed. New York: Macmillan Reference USA, 1999. Contains abbreviated information on a variety of health care careers.

Barbara Finkelstein, ed., *My First Year as a Nurse*. New York: Signet, 1997. Nineteen nurses tell their real-life nursing experiences during their first year as nurses.

Shirley H. Fondiller and Barbara J. Nerone, *Nursing: The Career of a Lifetime*. New York: National League of Nursing, 1995. A book explaining the field of nursing, published by a national organization that promotes nursing standards.

Jacqueline C. Kent, *Women in Medicine*. Minneapolis: Oliver, 1998. Contains stories profiling important female physicians, including a time line of women in medicine from 2500 B.C. to 1997.

Carol Kleiman, *The Hundred Best Jobs for the 1990s and Beyond*. Chicago: Dearborn Financial, 1992. Includes job requirements for several health care careers, including futuristic jobs and the top jobs.

Andrew Morkes, ed., *What Can I Do Now? Preparing for a Career in Nursing*. Chicago: Ferguson, 1998. An explanation of RNs' and LPNs' jobs and what it takes to succeed in those fields.

Melissa Ramsdell, ed., *My First Year as a Doctor*. New York: Walker, 1994. Each chapter contains a true story by a physician concerning what he or she learned during the first year of practice.

Barbara Swanson, *Careers in Health Care*. Lincolnwood, IL: VGM Career Horizons, 1995. This book covers fifty-eight health care careers, including lesser-known fields such as sports medicine, medical illustrator, dental lab technician, and dance therapist.

Periodicals

Health Care Professional Update, vol. 8, no. 2, *Houston Chronicle Supplement*, "HHS Report Finds Emerging Shortage of Licensed Pharmacists," February 2001.

Health Care Professional Update, vol. 8, no.2, *Houston Chronicle Supplement*, "US Medical School Applicants Still Exceed Available Positions," February 2001.

K. Pica Kahn, "Being a Paramedic Takes a Special Type of Person," *Health Care Professional Update*, vol. 8, no. 5, *Houston Chronicle Supplement*, May 2001.

———, "Therapists Work Hard to Keep Energized and Updated About Their Patients' Therapy Needs," *Health Care Professional Update*, vol. 8, no. 4, *Houston Chronicle Supplement*, April 2001.

Rosemary Luquire, "All Hospitals Can Do the Same to Attract Nurses," *Houston Chronicle*, August 27, 2001.

Cheryl L. Mee and Katherine W. Carey, "Nursing 2000 Salary Survey," *Nursing 2000*, vol. 30, no. 4, April 2000.

Internet Sources

AAMC Medical Education, "Community and Minority Programs," January 12, 2001. www.aamc.org/meded/minority/start.htm.

American Association of Colleges of Pharmacy, "Pharmacy School Admission Requirements 2001–02," 2000. www.aacp.org/Students/psar.html.

———, "How Do I Prepare for a Career in Pharmacy?" www.aacp.org/Students/How Do I Prepare.html.

American Association of Nurse Anesthetists, "The Cost Effectiveness of Nurse Anesthetist Practice," August 30, 2001. www.aana.com/crna/costeffect.asp.

American Heart Association, "CPR and AEDs," 2000. www.cpr-ecc.org/cpr_aed/cpr_aed_menu.htm.

American Medical Association, "A Comparison of Men and Women Physicians by Specialty, 1996 (table 6)." www.ama-assn.org/mem-data/wmmed/infoserv/data/table6.htm.

———, "Core Purpose," March 8, 2001. www.ama-assn.org/ama/pub/Category/1909.html.

———, "How We Work," March 8, 2001. www.ama-assn.org/ama/pub/Category/1815.html.

———, "Nathan Smith Davis, MD," March 20, 2001. www.ama-assn.org/ama/pub/article/1916-4389.html.

———, "Physicians by Gender (Excludes Students) (table 1)," 1997/1998. www.ama-assn.org/mem-data/wmmed/infoserv/data/table1.htm.

———, American Medical Association, "What We Do," March 8, 2001. www.ama-assn.org/ama/pub/category/1812.html.

———, "Women in US Medical Schools over a 20 Year Period (table 3)." www.ama-assn.org/mem-data/wmmed/infoserv/data/table3.htm.

———, "Women Physicians by Specialty (table 5)." www.ama-assn.org/mem-data/wmmed/infoserv/data/table5.html.

American Nurses Association, "Nursing Facts—Today's Registered Nurse—Numbers and Demographics," 1997. www.ana.org/readroom/Fsdemogr.htm.

American Physical Therapy Association, "Credentials of a Physical Therapist." www.mindspring.com/~wbrock/pttoday.htm.

———, "Current Annual Income (bar graph)," February 2000. www.apta.org/Research/survey_stat/pt_demo/pt_income.

———, "Employment Status (bar graph)," February 2000. www.apta.org/Research/survey_stat/pt_demo/pt_emp_status.

———, "Highest Earned Degree (bar graph)," February 2000. www.apta.org/Research/survey_stat/pt_demo/pt_hdegree.

———, "History and Introduction to Physical Therapy." www.mindspring.com/~wbrock/ptwhere.htm.

———, "History and Introduction to Physical Therapy," *Why Physical Therapy?* www.mindspring.com~wbrock/pthist.htm.

————, "Race/Ethnic Origin of Members (bar graph)," February 2000. www.apta.org/Research/survey_stat/pt_demo/pt_race.

————, "Sex (bar graph)," February 2000. www.apta.org/Research/survey_stat/pt_demo/pt_sex.

————,"Today's Physical Therapist." www.mindspring.com/~wbrock/pttoday.htm.

————, "Type of Facility in Which Members Practice (bar graph)," February 2000. www.apta.org/Research/survey_stat/pt_demo/pt_fac.

American Society of Clinical Pathologists, "Certification," January 22, 2001. www.ascp.org/bor/certification.

————, "Table 1. Hourly Median Pay Rates and Vacancy Rates for Laboratory Personnel by Workplace, Hospital Bed Size, and Region," 2001. www.ascp.org/bor/medlab/survey/98/table1.asp.

————, "The Medical Technologist (MT)," Careers in Medical Technology, April 26, 2000. www.ascp.org/bor/medlab/careers/page 2.asp.

————, "Preliminary Results of the 2000 Wage and Vacancy Survey of Medical Laboratories," December 14, 2000. www.ascp.org/bor/medlab/survey/00.

Association of American Medical Colleges, "AAMC Statement on Medical Education of Minority Group Students," January 30, 2001. www.aamc.org/meded/minority/recruit/statemin.htm.

————, "Careers in Medicine." www.aamc.org/students/considering/careers.htm.

————, "Getting into Medical School." www.aamc.org/students/considering/gettingin/htm.

————, "Making the Decision." www.aamc.org/students/considering/decision.htm.

BCM Pediatric Residency Program, "Rotations for Pediatric Residents." www.bcm.tmc.edu/pedi/res/content_08.html.

Deborah Belgum, "Stress, Horror of Job Mean High Level of Burnouts," Los Angeles Business Journal, November 8,1999. www.findarticles.com/m5072/45_21/57824439/p1/article.jhtml.

Bureau of Labor Statistics, "1998 National Occupational Employment and Wage Estimates," March 10, 2000. http://stats.bls.gov/oesnl/oes32902.htm.

Business Wire, "Response to Amtrak Derailment in Kansas," March 15, 2000. www.findarticles.com/cf_O/mOEIN/2000_March_15/6010070.../article.jhtml?term=EMT.

California Employment Development Department, "Labor Market Information—Physical Therapists," 1996. www.calmis/cahwnet.gov/file/occguide/PHYSTHER.HTM.

Career Guide to Industries, "Health Services," April 19, 2000. http://stats.bls.gov/oco/cg/cgs035.htm.

CareerZone, "Emergency Medical Technicians." www.explore.cornell.edu/newcareerzone/profile.asp?onet=32508.

CCS, Inc., "History of Defibrillation." www.defib.org/History.htm.

———, "Thirty-Five Years of CPR, What We Have Learned." www.defib.org/35_years_of_cpr.htm.

———, "What Is an AED?" www.defib.org/products.htm.

———, "What Is Sudden Cardiac Arrest?" www.defib.org/sudden_cardiac_arrest.htm.

City of Baton Rouge, "EMT Salaries," February 1997. www.ci.baton-rouge.la.us/DEPT/EMS/salary.htm.

Jeff Clet, "Years of Change, Years to Come," *9-1-1 Magazine,* 1999. www.9-1-1magazine.com/magazine/1999/0199/cols/ems.html.

Dennis V. Cookro, "The Community as a Public Health Patient—Reflections of a Public Health Specialist," *Jacksonville Medicine,* June 1998. www.dcmsonline.org/jax-medicine/1998journals/june1998/cookro.htm.

Robert A. DeLorenzo and Mark A. Eilers, "Lights and Siren: A Review of Emergency Vehicle Warning Systems," *Annals of Emergency Medicine,* 1991. www.medicalpriority.com/medical/articles/warningsystems1.htm.

"Emergency Medical Technicians." http://cbweb9p.collegeboard.org/career/bin/descrip.pl?num=102.

Federation of State Boards of Physical Therapy, "The Exam," 1997. www.fsbpt.org/exam5.htm.

———, "The Exam: About the Exam," 1997. www.fsbpt.org/exam.htm.

Amy Fletcher, "Workers for Med Labs in Short Supply," *Denver Business Journal,* July 13, 2001. http://denver.bcentral.com/denver/stories/2001/07/16/story4.html.

GeoCities, "The Story of Men in American Nursing." www.geocities. com/Athens/Forum/6011/sldoo1.htm.

Healthcare Career Resource Center, "Introduction." http://library. thinkquest.org/15569.

Health Resources and Services Administration, "Notes from the National Sample Survey of Registered Nurses," March 1996. http://bhpr.hrsa.gov/dn/survnote.htm.

————, "Selected Facts About Minority Registered Nurses," April 10, 2000. http://bhpr.hrsa.gov/dn/minority.htm.

Human Resources Development Canada, "Medical Laboratory Technologists, and Medical Radiation Technologists," 1997. www.nb.hrdc-drhc.gc.ca/common/1mi/job+/medica_1.html.

S. Ibister and S. Martinez, "Evolution of Hermann Life Flight in Houston," *Internet Journal of Aeromedical Transportation*, 2000. www.ispub.com/journals/IJAMT/Vol.1N2/life.html.

ICPAC, "Careers and Work—Physicians," July 2, 2001. http://icpac. indiana.edu/career_profiles?81120-3.html.

International Association of Medical Laboratory Technologists, "Home Page," March 16, 2001. www.iamlt.org/.

Kiwi Careers, "Personal Profile: Nalita Bali," February 8, 2001. www.careers.co.nz/jobs/3e_hte/j80133f.htm.

Robert Lowes, "What Do PA, NP, and CNM Spell? A Revolution in Healthcare," *Medical Economics Magazine*, March 20, 2000. www.findarticles.com/cf_dls/m3229/6_77/61537667/p.5/article. jhtml?term=.

Megan Malugani, "Job Q and A," Monster Healthcare, September 7, 2000. www.medsearch.com/qanda/jones.

Doreen Mangan, "Remember When . . . a Woman Doctor Was a Rarity? (Gender Discrimination Still Lives)," *Medical Economics Magazine*, May 11, 1998. www.findarticles.com/m3229/n9_v75/ 20853029/p1/article.jhtml.

Medscape, "Children Capable of Using Automated External Defibrillators," October 18, 1999. www.medscape.com/MedscapeWire/ 1999/10.99/medwire.1018.children.html.

Naples Daily News, "Basic Water Rescue," September 8, 1999. www.colliergov.net/ems/basic_water_rescue.htm.

National Registry for Emergency Medical Technicians, "About NREMT," 1997. www.nremt.org/aboutnremt.htm.

North Dakota Occupational Digest, "Medical Technologists." www.planningyourcareer.com/occupation_detail.asp.

NP Central, "NP Salary Summary," May 15, 2001. www.nurse.net/cgi-bin/start.cgi/salary/index.html.

NRMP, "About Residency," 2001. www.nrmp.org/res_match/about_res.

Occupational Outlook Handbook, "Clinical Laboratory Technologists and Technicians," December 14, 2000. http://stats.bls.gov/oco/ocos096.htm.

———, "Emergency Medical Technicians and Paramedics," October 2, 2000. http://stats.bls.gov/oco/ocos101.htm.

———, "Licensed Practical Nurses," October 2, 2000. www.bls.gov/oco/ocos102.htm.

———, "Occupations with Fast Growth and High Pay That Have the Largest Numerical Growth, Projected 1998–2008 (chart)." http://stats.bls.gov/oco/images/ocotjc08.gif.

———, "Pharmacists," July 30, 2000. http://stats.bls.gov/oco/ocos079.htm.

———, "Physical Therapist Assistants and Aides," December 14, 2000. http://stats.bls.gov/oco/ocos167.htm.

———, "Physical Therapists," July 17, 2000. www.bls.gov/oco/ocos080.htm.

———, "Physicians," July 14, 2000. http://stats.bls.gov/oco/ocos074.htm.

———, "Registered Nurses," July 14, 2000. http://stats.bls.gov/oco/ocos083.htm.

———, "Tomorrow's Jobs," April 19, 2000. http://stats.bls.gov/oco/oco2003.htm.

Elissa Osebold, "Paramedics Take the Plunge for Rescue Training," *Naples/Collier News*, September 8, 1999. www.colliergov.net/ems/basic_water_rescue.htm.

Paul Packard, "Life Flight," January 5, 2001. www.lifeflightweb.com/flight_crew.htm.

Pharmacy and You, "Pharmacists Licensure and Pharmacy Laws." www.pharmacyandyou.org/licensure/licensure.html.

"Pharmacy College Admission Test (PCAT)." www.gradview.com/testin/pcat.html.

"Physical Therapists." http://cbweb9p.collegeboard.org/career/bin/descrip.pl?num=081.

Physicians Search, "First Year Starting Salary—National Average," August 13, 2001. www.physicianssearch.com/physician/salary1.html.

———, "Physician Compensation Survey—in Practice Three Plus Years," August 13, 2001. www.physicianssearch.com/physician/salary2.html.

Ponca City News, "SJRMC Physical Therapy Provides Wound Care Plan," October 17, 1999. www.poncacitynews.com/News Archives/1099folder/10101799.html.

Rochester General Hospital, "What Are Medical Technologists?" www.viahealth.org/rgh/medical_technology/medtechs.htm.

Billi Rubin, "Phlebotomy Facts and Fun," 1999. www.svs.net/Later/home.htm.

SUNY at Stony Brook, "University Hospital Department of Emergency Medicine and the School of Health Technology and Management Health Sciences Center—Paramedic Program Schedule," 2000. www.informatics.sunysb.edu/emed/paramedic/2000-2~1.htm.

TBRNET, "Pathologist (Medical Ser.)." http://tbrnet.com/databases/jobtitles/0/070.061-010.shtml.

Texas Department of Public Safety, "Criminal Law Enforcement Crime Laboratory Service," 2000. www.txdps.state.tx.us/criminal_law_enforcement/crime_laboratory/index.htm.

Texas Nursing, vol. 74, no. 4, "Texas' Nursing Education System: Can It Respond to This Nursing Shortage?" April 2000. www.texshare.edu/ovidweb/ovidweb.cgi.

University of California, Los Angeles, "EMS Alumni." www.ucpd.ucla.edu/ucpd/ems/alumni.htm.

University of Texas Health Science Center, San Antonio, "Clinical Laboratory Technologists and Technicians." www.hetcat.uthscsa.edu/04020a54.html.

University of Texas Medical Branch, "1099—EMT Supervisor UTMB Managed Care," July 9, 2001. www.hr.utmb.edu/jobdesc/1xxx.jobc1099.htm.

University of Wisconsin, "History of Medical Technology." www.medsch.wisc.edu/education/medt/clsweb/coursesonline/CLS102/history.htm.

University of Wisconsin Medical Foundation, "Research Studies," 1999. www.uwdoctors.org/research/documents/research.htm.

U.S. Public Health Service, "Agencies with Pharmacists." www.os. dhhs.gov/progorg/pharmacy/agencies.html.

Wageweb, "Healthcare Salary Data," June 23, 2000. www.wageweb. com/health1.htm.

Roger Widmeyer, "Houston's EMS a Real Lifesaver," *Texas Medical Center News*, vol. 20, no. 3, February 15, 1998. www.tmc.edu/ tmcnews/02_15_98/page_02.html.

Workforce New Jersey Public Information Network, "Emergency Medical Technician." www.wnjpin.state.ng.us/OneStopCareer Center/JobSeeker/CareerFields/car0175.html.

Yahoo Careers, "Physicians." http://carcers.yahoo.com/employment/ oco/ocos074.html.

Jack Zackowski and Diane Powell, "The Future of Automation in Clinical Laboratories," *Medical Devicelink*, July 1999. www.device link.com/evdt/archive/99/07/010.html.

Index

physical therapists
  abilities needed for, 60–63
  advancement in careers of,
    66–68
  aides and assistants to, 62
  career potential in future for,
    70
  education of, 63–65, 68
  functions of, 58
  goals of, 58–63
  growth in field of, 58
  licensing examination for, 64
  patients of, 65–66
  qualities required for, 60–63
  rewards of, 63, 70
  salaries of, 68–70
  training for, 63–65
  women as, 68
  work environments of, 65–66,
    68
  work schedules of, 66
physical therapy aides, 62
  see also physical therapists
physical therapy assistants, 62
  see also physical therapists
physicians
  advancement in profession
    and, 40–41
  board certification of, 36
  continuing education and,
    41
  duties of, 28–30
  education of, 32–36, 41
  future job opportunities for,
    42–43
  government work opportuni-
    ties for, 38–39
  military service and, 40

  professional organization for, 30
  public health and, 40
  qualifications for, 31–32
  research and, 41
  rewards of, 43
  salaries of, 41–42
  women as, 39
  work environments available
    to, 36–38, 40
  work schedules of, 32, 38
  see also medical education;
    names of medical specialties
physiology, 34
police officers, 90, 93
prescription, 72
primary care physicians, 42
private practice, 37–38
psychiatry, 34, 36
PT (physical therapist), 65
  see also physical therapists
Public Health Service. See U.S.
  Public Health Service

radiology, 36, 42
registered nurses. see nurses, registered
rehabilitation, 58–63
research and, 81
RNs. See nurses, registered
robots, 56–57, 73
R.Ph. (registered pharmacist),
  78
  see also pharmacists

specialization. See medical or scientific field name; specific medical occupation
statistics, 11

Picture Credits

About the Author

Beverly Britton is a registered nurse with a diploma in nursing from St. Luke's Hospital School of Nursing, in Kansas City, Missouri; a B.S. in nursing from the University of Texas Health Science Center in Houston; and an M.S. in nursing from Texas Woman's University. In addition to working in numerous clinical nursing positions, she has been a professor of nursing at North Harris Montgomery Community College in Houston for twenty years. She lives in The Woodlands, Texas.

86-15413

306.8 Worth, Richard.
WOR
c.1   The American family

52011

THE
AMERICAN
FAMILY

THE
American
FAMILY

RICHARD WORTH

PHOTOGRAPHS BY ROBERT SEFCIK

A GROLIER COMPANY

FRANKLIN WATTS | 1984
NEW YORK | LONDON | TORONTO | SYDNEY

Photograph on page 51 courtesy of Josephine Jones

Library of Congress Cataloging in Publication Data

Worth, Richard.
The American family.

Bibliography: p.
Includes index.
Summary: Analyzes the role of the family in society,
and examines different types of families, including
single-parent families, unmarried couples living together,
and the traditional nuclear family.
1. Family—United States—Juvenile literature.
[1. Family. 2. Family life. 3. Family problems.
4. United States—Social life and customs] I. Title.
HQ536.W63   1984   306.8'5'0973   84-10369
ISBN 0-531-04859-4

52011

86-15413

CONTENTS

THE
AMERICAN
FAMILY

INTRODUCTION

For most Americans, the family brings to mind a variety of images that pass before us like photographs in an old, worn album.

- a young couple saying their marriage vows and promising to love each other for a lifetime.
- a mother cradling a tiny, newborn infant in her arms.
- a five-year-old child blowing out all the candles on his birthday cake.
- a freckle-faced girl with a long pigtail winning first prize at her school's science fair.
- two proud parents standing beside their son at his high school graduation.
- a white-haired grandfather pushing a stroller through the park in early spring.

These are all joyful images of the family . . . images we want to record and remember for years to come.

But unpleasant events occur in families too. Families can be the scene of bitter conflicts between a husband and wife that eventually lead to separation and divorce. They can be a battleground between parents and children, causing many children to run away from home never to set eyes on their parents again. And some children who are unfortunate enough to remain at home may become the victims of unspeakable cruelty and violence.

Yet, for better or for worse, the family is the most important institution in our lives. It shapes our values. It molds our views of the world. It forms the images we have of ourselves. The family is where we learn to love and to hate. It's where we learn our respect for humanity or our prejudices against others who are different from us. The family is where we learn what it means to be a woman or a man. The family is also our roots . . . our beginnings . . . our home . . . the source from which we can draw our strength to face whatever life holds in store for us.

No single volume can hope to cover every aspect of the family. It is a topic far too broad and too complex, one that touches on almost every aspect of our lives. For all of us are part of a family, and it influences so many of the things we do. Yet, in this book we will attempt to examine some of the most significant facets of the family. We will look at the way this important insititution is functioning in our society. We will also look at the many different types of families, such as single-parent families, unmarried couples living together, and the traditional nuclear family. Finally, we will seek to find the answers to a single, vital question: What is the condition of the American family today?

1

WHAT IS A FAMILY?

Throughout our history the meaning of the word *family* has changed. At various times the family has carried out different functions; family members have assumed different roles; and individuals have lived in a variety of family structures. While many of today's families might seem highly unusual to our colonial ancestors, they still contain important elements in common. Families past and present form a strong, unbroken bond that has made the American family an enduring tradition.

FAMILIES IN COLONIAL DAYS

The family has been a basic institution of American society since early colonial times. The Puritans, who came to Massachusetts in 1630, believed that the family provided strength and stability for their colony. In fact, they did everything possible to encourage single people to marry and have children. Single women were frowned on, and bachelors were taxed 20 shillings. Records show that the Puritan leaders were afraid that if a man remained single, his home might become a house of prostitution.

During the colonial period the vast majority of people married. Yet many colonists also remained single, largely because they couldn't find a mate. In the seventeenth century, for example, Maryland and Virginia reported that there weren't enough women available for all the men. At other times it may have been men who were in short supply because many were killed during the fierce conflicts with the French and Indians in the seventeenth and eighteenth centuries.

The English colonists were not the only ones who suffered from a shortage of mates; their enemies, the French in Canada, faced the same problem. The French government in Paris even took to sending over shiploads of eligible young women so all the men in the colony could marry. But women were still too few in number. The Comte de Frontenac, Canada's most illustrious governor-general in the seventeenth century, wrote: "If a hundred and fifty girls . . . had been sent out this year, they would all have found husbands and masters within a month."

Throughout the colonial era Americans generally married later in life than they do today. The average age for a man was 25. At this age a man frequently owned a farm or had established himself in a craft or business. He was then in a position to support a wife and children. Older men were also considered more mature, pious, and hard-working—qualities essential in a desirable husband.

Women married somewhat later too, the average age being about 23 or older. Suitable brides were expected to have much the same qualities as their husbands. One other trait was also necessary—obedience. Among the well-to-do it was important to have the approval of one's parents before marrying. If a father was wealthy and planning to give his son or daughter some property, he might change his mind if he didn't approve of that son's or daughter's spouse.

In the latter part of the colonial period, another quality became increasingly important in selecting a mate: sexual attractiveness. But our ancestors never believed that anyone should be foolish enough to marry simply on the basis of sexual attractiveness and romantic love.

When people married in colonial America, it was usually for keeps. Divorce was almost unheard of. The rigid divorce laws were certainly a primary reason. These laws were supported by custom and religious teaching and remained largely unchallenged by the masses of people. Our ancestors placed a very high value on the institution of marriage. Preserving that institution seemed far more important than whether or not an individual found personal happiness within marriage. If an individual made an unhappy marriage, he or she was expected to make the best of it. There was also a very practical reason to keep a marriage going. Couples living on the frontier needed to stay together to survive. Life was a daily struggle against the wilderness, the weather, and the hostile Indians: People had to depend on each other.

Some individuals, however, were so unhappy living together that they could not endure it. Newspaper articles from the period refer to husbands and wives who ran away from home to seek a better life. For others, only death proved a final escape. The tombstone of Virginia councillor John Custis, who died more than two hundred years ago, reads:

> Aged 71 years, and yet lived but seven years, which was the space of time he kept a bachelor's home at Arlington on the Eastern Shore of Virginia.

We often look back nostalgically to the colonial period as a time when many families consisted of parents, children, and grandparents often living together. But these *extended families,* as they are called, were in a small minority. The vast majority of family units in the past, just as today, were *nuclear families.* These consisted of a mother, father, and their children.

It is not really surprising that nuclear families were so common among a population where few people lived long enough to become grandparents. The nuclear family structure also appealed to a hearty, colonial people who placed great importance on self-sufficiency. As sons grew up, they were often impatient to leave home and move westward. There land was available and they could establish their own homesteads just as their fathers had done.

Colonial families were generally larger than the small nuclear families of today. A woman might give birth to seven or eight children, although some generally died in infancy. Lacking adequate measures of birth control, a woman began childbearing early in her married life. And for some it ended tragically in the pain of childbirth. During this period it was not uncommon for people to marry two or even three times due to the death of their spouses. The result might be enormous families with ten or more children.

The family in colonial America functioned as a productive unit that depended on the work of many hands. Although the husband was primarily responsible for supporting his family, husbands and wives often worked together in the fields, or in running a store or inn. A wife might also tend a garden, make clothing for her family, and even produce extra clothes to be bartered or sold. Husbands often helped their wives with domestic chores and childrearing. As children grew older, they were expected to help their parents: boys took their place alongside their fathers, and girls beside their mothers.

Colonial parents considered their children more than just a source of free labor, however. They were also concerned that children be given the proper upbringing. To the Puritans, for example, children represented the future. They would carry on and run the society that their parents had started. Cotton Mather, the Puritan clergyman, praised these children. "The Youth in this Country are verie Sharp," he said, "and early Ripe in their Capacities."

The Puritans loved their children, but they did not demonstrate much affection for fear of spoiling them. Instead, Puritan parents thought that it was in the best interests of their children to be strict and often harsh with them. In this way children would develop a strong sense of self-discipline, as well as other positive traits such as piety, sobriety, and industriousness.

Many colonial parents also tried to provide children with a basic education. For the most part, this consisted of a little training at home in the "3Rs"—reading, writing, and arithmetic. In New England, however, many towns established schools where children sat from early morning until late afternoon having the basics drilled into them. While children recited their lessons, they were also learning Puritan theology. A stanza from the New England Primer goes:

> *In* Adam's *fall*
> *We sinned all.*
>
> *Thy life to mend,*
> *God's* Book *attend.*

For most young people who grew up during the colonial period, childhood was short. If children were not working alongside their parents at an early age, they were often apprenticed to a craftsman to learn a trade. Benjamin Franklin, for example, left school at the age of 10 to assist his father, a soapmaker. At age 12, he was apprenticed to his half brother, the publisher of the *New England Courant,* where Ben learned the printing trade.

A small number of boys might hope for more formal education offered by the "grammar" schools, similar to our high schools. And a very few might even be as fortunate as John Adams and attend Harvard College.

In summary, the typical family in colonial America was a nuclear family. The ultimate authority in each family lay with the husband/father, who was supposed to be the sole provider. In practice, however, husbands and wives and, later, children shared this task in order to make the family as productive as possible. As well as being a unit of production (that is, producing goods for the family's use) the family fulfilled a variety of other functions. It provided an intimate relationship for a man and a woman. It gave them and their children affection and emotional support. The family also provided children with care, socialization (training in the values and beliefs of the community), vocational skills, and an education. Family members provided their own protection against outside enemies. Most of the leisure activities enjoyed by children and adults occurred inside the family. Finally, the family acted as a launching pad, sending children out into the world.

In short, no other institution in colonial America was more versatile or expected to do as much as the family.

THE CHANGING FAMILY

During the nineteenth century, Americans continued moving across the continent, pushing back the frontier until eventually they had reached the Pacific Ocean. Thousands of families moved west, seeking a better life, just as their ancestors had done in earlier centuries. They cleared the land, built homes, fought insects, drought, and hostile Indians, and finally succeeded in establishing permanent settlements. Here the family continued to function much as it had during the colonial period. Families were the basic institution of every rural community, providing the strength and stability that held it together.

But within those eastern cities that the settlers had left behind events were occurring that would change the family forever. America had begun its Industrial Revolution.

Little by little people were being drawn off the land to new jobs that were opening up in factories and offices. Leaving before sunrise and often arriving home after dark, men now spent the day separated from the rest of their families. These families now ceased to be units of production; this function was taken over by industry.

Husbands and wives also stopped working together. While a husband went off to his job, his wife remained behind to run the household. She was now solely responsible for domestic chores and carried the burden of child-rearing. Although the man continued to hold ultimate authority in the family, the home became exclusively a woman's domain. Here she was usually in charge.

During the nineteenth century, industrialization increasingly separated the man's world from the woman's world, and the family from the workplace. As the workplace grew more mechanized and impersonal, the family became more important as a place to retreat. Within his family a man was more than simply a cog in a giant machine; he could feel valued as a husband and father. The family provided a safe harbor, removed from the daily grind of the factory, where a man might hope to enjoy satisfying personal relationships and find comfort. Women were the guardians of the family. They were expected to create a warm, supportive atmosphere for their husbands and children. Women were admired and loved for their important roles as care-givers and mothers. But it was understood that women—at least in the middle and upper classes—would remain at home to fulfill these roles and not venture into the man's world of the workplace.

Throughout the period childhood often ended at an early age as youth left home to learn a useful trade. Some parents continued to apprentice their children as in the past. Horace Greeley, founder of the *New York Tribune*, was apprenticed at age 15 to a printer in Vermont. Other youth received a more informal, on-the-job training. John D. Rockefeller went to work as a bookkeeper at age 16 when his family moved outside Cleveland. And financier Jay Cooke worked for a transport company. Many poor children had to settle for jobs in the factories. By 1890, there were nearly 2 million children between the ages of 10 and 15 at work, not only in factories, but also in a variety of other jobs such as peddlers, ragpickers, and newsboys.

Americans saw nothing wrong with child labor. It had existed for centuries and seemed to follow from the Puritan ethic, which decreed that people should work hard if they wanted to get ahead. Popular novels, such as those of Horatio Alger, portrayed poor boys who persevered and became successful. The career of John D. Rockefeller proved that success and great wealth were more than just the stuff of fiction.

Yet many middle-class parents were beginning to believe that something other than simple hard work was necessary for their children to succeed. Society had become more complex and the competition was increasing. There might be a great success story such as Rockefeller's, but for every one of these there were at least a hundred failures. Parents were looking for a way to insure that their children didn't fail, to equip them with the necessary skills to find a job in an age when jobs were becoming increasingly specialized and technical.

Education seemed to be the answer. Large companies were looking for people with formal education. And a formal program of instruction was also necessary to enter the professions, which seemed to offer a youth the best chance of success.

During the nineteenth century, states began to establish a system of free public elementary schools. Gradually, high schools were established too, although only about 10 percent of the nation's young people actually attended them in 1900. This number would grow to 50 percent by the 1930s, with an ever-increasing number of students continuing their education in college.

A program of formal education that began in elementary school and extended at least through high school seemed to solve some serious problems that troubled many parents. One of these was what they should do with their children during adolescence. In 1904, G. Stanley Hall had drawn attention to this period with the publication of his famous work, *Adolescence.* This was a difficult period when youth were neither children nor adults and they could easily take the wrong path in life unless they received the proper training.

Parents may have felt inadequate to provide this training themselves and felt the need of experts to help them. The experts agreed. As one educator stated in 1910, the school was "fast taking the place of the home, not because it wishes to do so, but because the home does not fulfill its functions." Presumably the family, at least according to some experts, was turning out too many failures and misfits.

During the nineteenth century the family's functions were gradually reduced. Although the majority of Americans still lived in rural areas, more and more people were moving to the cities and working in industry. As a result of this, many families now produced little or nothing inside the home. Instead, they were primarily consumers who purchased products that were produced elsewhere.

The Industrial Revolution affected the family in other ways, too. The home and the workplace were now separated, and the roles of husband and wife became more distinct. The family's role in training and educating its children was gradually being taken over by the schools, which seemed to provide the education necessary to fill jobs in industry. Young people would now remain in school longer. This meant that they would also stay at home longer and remain dependent on their parents for a longer period of time. These changes would greatly affect the family in the years ahead.

THE FAMILY IN
THE TWENTIETH CENTURY

Around the turn of the century some family life experts were saying that the American family was in the midst of a grave crisis. It had lost some of its most important functions. The experts also pointed out that divorce rates were climbing slowly upward, while the birth rates were declining. In addition, more women seemed to be entering the work force instead of staying at home and raising children. After looking at these developments, one commentator was moved to write:

> Young women are gradually being imbued with the idea that marriage and motherhood are not to be their chief objects in life . . . that housekeeping is a sort of domestic slavery. If this view is correct, the birth-rate will not only continue low in the United States compared to former years, but it will probably become lower.

Birthrates did continue to decline during the early years of the twentieth century, as this commentator feared. Nevertheless, the marriage rates remained relatively unchanged. Most people were probably no less interested in having families; they just wanted smaller ones.

In fact, the twentieth century in America has sometimes been called the Century of the Child, because society seemed more interested than ever before in the proper upbringing of children. Psychologists, such as Sigmund Freud, pointed out the importance of the early childhood years to an individual's future development. A much greater emphasis was also being placed on a child's education. By the 1920s, most states prohibited children from working before the age of 16 and required them to stay in school. At the same time, elementary education was becoming more rigorous, and a larger percentage of students were finishing high school and attending college.

If ours has been called the Century of the Child, then the era following World War II was surely the Golden Era of the Family. American GIs returning home in 1945 hoped to put the nightmare of war behind them and resume lives that had been so cruelly interrupted. To millions, this included getting married, settling down, and raising children. American women had the same idea.

The years after the war witnessed an increase in the marriage rate. Women started getting married earlier, too. The average age of marriage declined to just over 20 in 1956, with many women marrying in their teens. Births in the United States increased, too. Rising gradually after the war, the number of births shot past the 4 million mark in 1954 and stayed there for ten years.

The 75 million Americans born between 1946 and 1964 are known as the baby boom generation. This was an era of tremendous prosperity in the United States, quite a change for most parents who had lived through the hardships of the Great Depression. These parents were generally in agreement that their children should not have to suffer as they did. They wanted their kids to have the best of everything. As author Landon Y. Jones points out in his book *Great Expectations:* "They would have more toys, more money, and more attention."

During this era the role of parents underwent important changes. These were often reflected by the media in magazines, books, and in such popular television series as *Father Knows Best*. Gone were the days when father was a stern authority figure; now he was more a friend. Parents believed that they should provide their children with as much warmth, affection, and understanding as possible. Parents also tried to instill in their children a desire to question and think for themselves, while all the time reassuring them that they had the ability to make the right decisions. Sometimes it appeared not that father knew best, but that his children did.

During the 1950s and 1960s, many individuals of the baby boom generation reached their adolescence. Their sheer numbers were enormous—there were 22 million teenagers in 1964—and most of them were crowding into junior high and high schools throughout America. Here, largely cut off from contact with the adult world, they began to form their own youth culture. No longer did they look so much to parents and teachers for guidance and leadership, but to other teenagers in their peer group. Youth had their own slang, their own clothing styles, their own music, their own heroes.

Middle-class youth, who had been taught by their parents to question and had been constantly reassured that they knew best, now began to question almost everything. Within the family children challenged their parents' authority and their values. Although a generation gap has probably always existed between parents and children, it seemed to grow wider during the 1960s.

In many cases, young people now appeared to be leading their parents rather than the other way around.

THE SEXUAL REVOLUTION

Youth were among the leaders of an enormous change in sexual values, known as the Sexual Revolution. For centuries Americans believed that sexual relations should be restricted to marriage and should be for the sole purpose of producing children. There were exceptions, of course. Men were permitted, even encouraged, to have sexual experiences before marriage, and were even allowed occasional infidelities by their wives. Women—at least "pure" women—were never permitted these things. This so-called "double standard" had existed in Western society at least since the days of the ancient Hebrews. Women were expected to be virgins at the time of their marriage—and remain faithful during marriage—so their husbands could be sure that any offspring were legitimate. This was especially important when land was being passed on from one generation to the next.

These traditional values have changed during the past two decades. New methods of birth control have freed women from the fear of becoming pregnant as a result of intercourse. For the first time sexual relations have been separated from the production of children. Today sexual intercourse is valued for the feelings of pleasure and intimacy it can provide a couple as well as for the children that might be produced.

The effects of the Sexual Revolution on the family will be discussed throughout this book. Briefly stated, it has changed dating patterns and engagement periods. The Sexual Revolution has led to an increase in the number of people living together without marriage. It has also led couples to expect greater sexual satisfaction in their marriage relationships; and when this has not happened, they have been more likely to divorce.

THE WOMEN'S MOVEMENT

While the sexual revolution was underway, the family was being affected by another dynamic force: the Women's Movement. To understand how this movement developed, a brief background might be helpful.

As you may recall, during the colonial period women had taken on a variety of roles. Aside from running a home and raising a family, they often worked side by side with their husbands in the fields. Women also ran inns, and some even worked as shipwrights, blacksmiths, and millers.

In the nineteenth century, industrialization separated the man's world and the woman's world. Middle-class women were expected to stay at home and fill the roles of wife, mother, and housewife. Lower-class women, of course, were not so restricted; they frequently had to work to help support their families. Still, as late as mid-century, married women had no legal rights to their wages and no property rights. They were completely controlled by their husbands.

A few women raised their voices in protest. In 1848, at the first Women's Rights Convention held in Seneca Falls, New York, feminists issued a declaration that stated: "We hold these truths to be self-evident: that all men and women are created equal." Gradually, married women won rights to such things as property and wages; and finally with the passage of the 19th amendment in 1920, women won the right to vote.

Although an increasing number of women were entering the workplace to pursue careers, most remained at home. Women had generally been brought up to believe that a family offered them love and security, while a career meant that they must spend their lives alone. Unlike men, women could not have both a career and a family.

The Second World War, however, presented women with an unusual opportunity. With so many men needed to fight in Europe and the Pacific, a large number of jobs suddenly opened up at home. Women were the only ones available to fill them, and millions joined the work force. But after the war ended and the men came back, many women gave up their jobs and went home. The period following the war became the Golden Era of the American Family.

In her book *The Feminine Mystique,* published in 1963, Betty Friedan wrote that American society was telling women that they should be content with the life of the suburban housewife. She had a beautiful home with all the modern appliances, and her major function was to serve her husband and children. Many women believed that they could find fulfillment in this lifestyle, this "feminine mystique." While interviewing some of them, however, Friedan found that they felt bored and empty; and one after another reported that life seemed to hold very little meaning for her.

Friedan believed that the mystique prevented women from establishing an identity apart from someone's wife or mother. She went on to say:

> Women, as well as men, can only find their identity in work that uses their full capacities. A woman cannot find her identity through others. . . . She cannot find it in the dull routine of housework . . . American women [must] break out of the housework trap and truly find fulfillment as wives and mothers—by fulfilling their own unique possibilities as separate human beings.

Friedan's book helped begin the Women's Movement that continues today. Her words not only struck a responsive chord among housewives, but also among the millions of women who were already in the labor force. During the next two decades many more women entered the workplace; women created new roles for themselves; relationships between women and men underwent important changes; and the roles of men changed too.

These developments have had a great impact on the family. Briefly stated, women now have more options

*The changing roles of men and
women have brought a new dimension
to the American family.*

available to them and a far greater degree of independence. They may choose not to marry; and if they do marry, the role of housewife and mother is no longer the only one open to them. Finally, women no longer feel bound to remain in an unsatisfying marriage—they can leave with the assurance that they will be able to support themselves. We will look at these developments in greater detail in succeeding chapters.

PAST TO PRESENT

From the earliest colonial days until the present, the American family has demonstrated both continuity and change. Here are some examples.

The overwhelming majority of Americans have always married. During the colonial period, people married during their mid-20s. Today men marry, on average, at about age 25 and women are usually over the age of 22—older than the average age of marriage during the 1950s, but about the same as our colonial ancestors. More women are postponing marriage at present to finish college and begin careers. The later age at which people marry may also reflect their uncertainty about the current state of the economy and their ability to find well-paying jobs.

The family is smaller now than in the past, the average family being about 2.75 people. In part, this is because families have fewer children. This is much easier because of the effectiveness of modern birth control methods. Many married women are also postponing the age at which they have children to pursue careers. Among more than 50 percent of married couples, wives are working outside the home, something that might be considered a substantial victory for the Women's Movement. Although some women leave the workplace once they have children, many others continue working, though often only part time.

Today more and more people live in families that are not nuclear family units. For example, there are over 8 million single-parent families headed by women. In large part this is due to the high number of divorces in America, which has risen steadily throughout this century. For every two marriages in the United States, there is presently one divorce, bringing the total of divorced people to about 11 million. We'll look more closely at the reasons for divorce and its effects in Chapters 4 and 5.

Another type of family consists of an unmarried couple living together. There are now more than 2 million of these couples, almost four times the number in 1970. This is a reflection of our more liberal sexual values.

Today, there are also many more older married couples, resulting from major advances in medicine that keep more people living longer. As one member of the couple, generally the husband, dies, the other is left alone. Today there are 12.8 million widowed people, the majority of them over the age of 65. In Chapter 6 we'll look at the impact of death, as well as widowhood, on the family.

Perhaps the greatest changes in the family over the centuries have been its functions. No longer do families produce the necessities of life; now they are consumers who purchase their food, clothing, and other items. Although the family is still responsible for raising children, much of this responsibility has been taken over by other institutions, such as the school. The government is primarily responsible for providing the family with protection; the government also helps families with welfare payments when they are unable to support themselves. Most of the leisure activities a family enjoys are not created at home but produced by outside sources such as toy manufacturers or television networks.

What, then, is the function of the family in today's world? It is primarily to provide its members with affection, understanding, and intimate relationships; and to give them an opportunity to share their lives together. No other institution in the history of humankind has ever accomplished these tasks as successfully; nor is any likely to. This is the reason that the family continues to endure.

It is important to realize, however, that these tasks can be carried out effectively in a variety of family groups. There is no single type of unit that constitutes a family. A family may be a father and his adopted child; a divorced woman and her children; two parents and their children; an unmarried couple who live together; or children, parents, and grandparents, all living under the same roof.

As we look at the American family today—its functions and its various forms—we can propose a definition of the family that may prove useful throughout the remainder of this book. It is the definition developed by the American Home Economics Association.

Two or more persons who share resources, share responsibility for decisions, share values and goals, and have commitments to one another over a period of time. The family is that climate that one comes home to; and it is that network of sharing and commitments that most accurately describes the family unit, regardless of blood, legalities, adoption or marriage.

2

THE FAMILY CYCLE

Over the past 350 or more years the American family as an institution has undergone a variety of changes. Similarly an individual family undergoes many changes throughout its lifetime. These changes are known as the family cycle.

Like a human being, a human family proceeds from birth, through childhood and maturity, to old age and death.

A new family unit begins when two people form a relationship and make a commitment to each other over a period of time. The commitment generally involves marriage, although in some situations marriage is not involved. The majority of married couples have one or more children. The coming of children expands the family and produces the greatest change in a family unit. Gradually, children mature and their parents grow older, creating new stresses and strains. Eventually the children leave home to establish their own lives; and the original family now shrinks in size, reduced to only two adults once again. Finally, death claims one of the spouses, leaving the remaining spouse and his or her children, who still form a type of extended family.

Of course, the life cycle of many families is not always so simple. It may be broken along the way by divorce, or by the untimely death of a parent or child. Adult children may also decide to move back home to live with their parents for an extended stay. Nevertheless, the life cycle provides a useful model that helps us to examine the family at different stages and recognize the changes that are occurring.

In this chapter and the next we will look at these stages. Then in the following chapters we will focus on two events that can break the family cycle: divorce and the death of a parent.

BEGINNING A RELATIONSHIP

The way in which young people meet and form relationships has changed dramatically over the centuries. During the colonial period a boy and girl may not have been permitted to begin dating unless their parents approved. Then the couple were given very little chance to be alone. If they went out, they would quite likely be chaperoned; and if they stayed home, it was at the girl's home in the presence of her parents.

By the early twentieth century, however, young people were growing up in a different environment. High schools were bringing more adolescents together and giving them greater contact with each other while the movie theater and the automobile gave them a greater opportunity to be alone.

For many years dating had often followed an established pattern. A boy asked a girl out and usually paid for everything. If the couple enjoyed being together, they would start "going steady" and eventually get married. Today dating patterns are frequently different. Groups of students in high school or college often "hang out" together, although some may eventually pair off. In addition, a young woman might ask a man out on a date; and a couple frequently shares expenses.

The choice of people with whom to form relationships is generally influenced by a variety of factors. One of these is convenience: how easy it is to see another person. Take Julie and Bob, for example. They went out during their last two years of high school; and when each went away to a different college, they promised to write every day and to see each other as often as possible. At first, the letters did come daily. Then, once a week. And finally, hardly at all. It had become too difficult for Julie and Bob to maintain a long-distance relationship. Meanwhile they had met other people in their own colleges with whom they were developing new relationships. As someone once said: "Absence makes the heart grow fonder, but often for somebody else."

If we tend to form most of our associations with people who are nearby, how do we then select from all of them, that one person with whom to have a close, special relationship? One criterion is an individual's physical appearance. In fact, this is often the first thing that attracts us. Also, we generally want the person to share our interests—whether it's rock music, water-skiing, or old Charlie Chaplin films. In addition, many people feel more comfortable if they're going with someone who has the approval of their friends, if not their parents.

Today young men and women generally enter into a number of relationships with each other before marriage. Frequently they will confront the issue of whether or not to engage in sexual intercourse—a decision that will depend upon their values. As we saw in the last chapter, the Sexual Revolution of the 60s and 70s had enormous impact on our views about sex. Nevertheless, some people continue to believe strongly that they should not have sexual relations until they are married. Others still subscribe to a "double standard" for males and females. However, the Women's Movement has demanded an end to the double standard and equality for both sexes in a relationship, something now made possible by effective methods of birth control.

The availability of birth control devices, however, has not prevented a large number of teenagers from giving birth illegitimately. Between 1970 and 1980, the number of these births among teenagers jumped from about 200,000 to 274,000 annually. This has probably resulted from greater sexual activity among teenagers; and a greater willingness to report illegitimate births because society now accepts them more readily. Among black teenagers the illegitimacy rate is much higher than among whites. Eighty-six percent of the births among black teenagers are illegitimate as compared to 33 percent among whites. One reason, according to experts, is that blacks seem to have less hope for the future—with few prospects for a good education or good jobs.

Once a teenager becomes pregnant and gives birth, she will probably leave school. Some may marry the fathers of their children, but many will not and will remain single parents. Either way, their prospects for the future often grow even bleaker, with little chance for more education, a fulfilling job, or a stable marriage.

Of course, the majority of American teenagers avoid this fate, although a large number of them probably engage in sex. On college campuses many students now believe that sexual intercourse can become a meaningful part of a relationship whenever two people love each other. Critics charge, however, that these sexual values lead to promiscuous behavior. Young people, they say, now justify sexual intercourse by simply saying "I love you." This results in a series of short-term relationships, the critics contend, in which young people only try to satisfy their own sexual needs and don't really care about the other person in the relationship.

Other experts point out that while some young people have acted irresponsibly, many others have shown a great deal of responsibility in their relationships. Young people, these experts say, recognize that it is up to them to honestly evaluate their own feelings toward one another and to be truthful in expressing these feelings.

Further, the experts contend, young people seem to realize that sexual relations involve a commitment to another person that cannot be taken lightly. Finally, many of these young people have been capable of forming relatively long-term relationships, which have included cohabitation and marriage.

COHABITATION

Today more than 2 million couples live together without being married, an arrangement that is called cohabitation. Many of these couples are college students. College provides a relaxed atmosphere where young people are generally free to experiment and try new relationships.

For some students who feel affection for each other, living together has become a convenient arrangement that seems to have replaced "going steady."

Other people see living together as a form of "trial marriage." For these couples, living together may be the first step toward getting married, if they feel that their relationship is satisfying. These couples point out that many marriages fail because people do not really know each other before marriage. This problem can be avoided, they say, by first living with another person; then if the couple decides to marry, the marriage will be a more satisfying experience. Yet studies show that living together seems to have little effect on marriage. Married couples who had first lived together seemed to be no happier than those who had not. However, living arrangements may give couples an opportunity to recognize any major problems that they have in their relationship and to avoid marriages that might end in disaster.

For some people, living together is not a first step toward marriage, but a definite alternative. As one man in a living arrangement explained:

I was married for six years, then divorced. And the entire experience was very unpleasant for me.

Since then, I've had a relationship with another woman for five years. We love each other very much and I don't want to do anything that might wreck that. Neither one of us wants children, so there's no need to get married for that reason. I realize that the problem when I was married may have been that the relationship just wasn't right. But I'm also afraid that it might have been the institution of marriage. Maybe marriage just isn't for me. Living together seems different. I feel freer somehow. I can be myself.

Are living arrangements really different from marriage? Some writers have pointed out that people in them tend to place greater emphasis on themselves instead of the relationship. According to one study, cohabiting couples expressed as much commitment to each other as engaged couples, but less than married couples.

Another study suggests that individuals in living arrangements are more likely than married couples to recognize each other's need for privacy and individuality. In short, there seems to be less emphasis on togetherness than in the traditional marriage. Yet couples in living arrangements also report being overinvolved with each other and cut off from relationships with other people. They commonly say: "I feel trapped" or "I feel like I'm married."

Finally, people in a living arrangement often point out that one of the great advantages over marriage is that you can leave much more easily. While there may not be any legal separation or divorce, individuals who break up after living together do nevertheless suffer from emotional separation and a deep sense of loss.

In sum, many living arrangements may not be much different from marriage. And whether or not they are satisfying seems to depend less on the structure of the relationship than on the people involved in it—their maturity, their ability to care for each other and to recognize each other's needs.

PREPARING TO MARRY

The vast majority of adults—more than 90 percent—get married. Many people marry out of a desire to share their lives with another person, as well as a desire to have children together. For others, marriage may also provide a way to escape from an unhappy home, a method of avoiding loneliness and an opportunity to satisfy their need for security.

In a period of high divorce, those people who are planning marriage are especially anxious to avoid becoming another divorce statistic. While no marriage is guaranteed success, there are a few things to consider that will have a strong impact on the future of the relationship:

1. *Your sense of self.* Do you know who you are and what's important to you? Do you have a positive self-image?

2. *Compatibility.* Do you and your mate have a similar philosophy of life? Do you have similar interests? Do you have similar needs to be alone and to be with other people? Do you have similar feelings about having children? About money?

3. *Roles.* Do you and your mate have similar views on your roles as husband and wife? Examples: Should a wife have a career? Should she stop work to raise children? Should a husband be the primary breadwinner? Should he have equal responsibility for raising children?

4. *Communication.* How well do you express your needs? How willingly do you listen to your mate?

How successful are you at working out disagreements?

5. *Flexibility.* People change during a relationship and relationships change. Satisfying marriages require flexibility on the part of both partners.

It may be difficult to confront these issues during the weeks and months preceding marriage. While a couple is dating or engaged, they usually strive to present themselves as favorably as possible. A woman may try to be witty and charming even if she feels in a bad mood. A man may try to appear knowledgeable and decisive even when he isn't always sure of himself. Both may believe that this is what's expected of them . . . what the other wants. They may also try to overlook any areas where they are not really compatible. She may not like the fact that he spends too much money and he may think that she drinks too much. But each may be afraid of criticizing the other for fear of ending the relationship. And they often try to convince themselves that somehow these problems will be resolved after the marriage.

For a small number of couples, however, some issues seem far too important to be postponed until after the wedding day. To reduce any possibility of misunderstanding that might later result in divorce, they draw up an antenuptual (before the wedding) agreement. These agreements often deal with property rights. For instance, a man and woman may agree that any property either one owned before the marriage will remain hers or his alone and will not be owned jointly. Antenuptual agreements have also defined such things as a couple's responsibility for raising children and financially supporting the household as well as the division of household labor.

When a couple marry, they make a commitment to each other. This commitment is not only legally binding; it may involve a religious ceremony too. In the past these ceremonies followed a set format, and all couples exchanged similar vows. These included words like "love," "honor," and "obey." But today, more and more couples are modifying these ceremonies and the vows to suit themselves.

Other couples choose not to marry in a formal religious ceremony. Recently a young couple got married at a nature preserve in front of 100 of their closest friends. The couple created their own ceremony, which included statements of their feelings toward each other and original music composed and played by one of their guests.

These public rituals are very important. They give notice to the community that a couple have made a commitment to each other. The community acts as a witness to this commitment. The community reinforces the commitment and makes it more solid. Two people are probably less likely to fall out of a relationship when everyone knows about it.

THE FIRST YEARS
OF MARRIAGE

One of the problems reported by many young married couples is that marriage isn't what they expected it would be. This generally happens because their expectations were unrealistic. For example, some people get married believing that they should agree on everything. At the first sign of any serious disagreement, a husband or wife may feel betrayed. "You don't love me," one of them might say. "If you did, you'd do what I want." Obviously, no married couple should expect to agree all the time. Yet, if one or both partners have a negative self-image, a disagreement may be especially hard to take. They can easily see a disagreement as a form of criticism, overreact to it, and not try to work it out.

It is quite natural, of course, that married couples will have differences. One of these may be a different

*The wedding ritual is an important
event in the life of the family.*

need for closeness—touching, intimacy, and expressions of affection. It may just be that one person needs more time to be alone than another . . . more space . . . more freedom. Yet, this person may also fear too much intimacy. People who have not established a strong sense of self are often afraid of losing their identities if they become too close to another.

Problems such as this often come to the surface only after a marriage begins. During the engagement period, they may have been carefully hidden or overlooked, or they may not have seemed so bad because the couple wasn't together all the time.

Carrie and Jim, for example, have been married about three months. While they were going out together, Jim realized that Carrie was very close to her mother and consulted her about almost everything. Jim told himself that this situation would probably change after he and Carrie were married and had their own life together. But after the marriage the situation remained the same. Carrie's mother helped them select all the furniture for their new apartment. And she would "drop over" for dinner at least two or three times a week. When Jim had suggested that Carrie speak to her mother, she immediately refused and accused him of trying to come between a mother and daughter.

"I made no secret of how much Mom means to me when we were going out together," Carrie said.

And, indeed, she hadn't. But the relationship didn't seem so bad when Jim wasn't living with it every day.

Jim had married one woman and now found himself with two.

Many newly married people who have found themselves in Jim's situation have probably wondered "What have I gotten myself into?" Problems that go unresolved in the early years of marriage will generally grow worse as time goes on. And only when a couple is willing to communicate can important issues, such as the one that confronted Jim and Carrie, be resolved.

—33—

Communication is extremely important during the early years of marriage, because a couple has so many important tasks to accomplish. These frequently include establishing a home together and getting used to living with each other on a daily basis. Since most women work after they are married, wives and husbands must also handle the demands of each other's jobs. Couples must determine who is responsible for the variety of duties that are part of running a household, such as cleaning, grocery shopping, and bill paying. Finally, married couples are expected to maintain friendly relations with their in-laws.

Sometimes these tasks conflict. For example, a woman may have been looking forward to spending a quiet weekend at home with her husband. But, instead, they must attend a wedding anniversary party for his parents. Or a wife's career may be so demanding that she may not be able to do her share of the household chores. At times like this, a young couple need to be flexible, understanding, and willing to compromise.

PREPARATION FOR PARENTHOOD

Perhaps the most important change that occurs in a family is the coming of children. The birth of a child will bring a third person into the family. The close relationship between a husband and wife must now expand to include someone else. And with this new life, a couple must share the love, the care, and the time they had reserved only for each other.

Today, couples can choose whether to have children. This option was not open to people in past centuries because birth control methods were usually ineffective. In addition, it has now become acceptable for a couple to remain childless, a choice that was frowned on only a few years ago. Some couples are simply not interested in having children. Certainly without them a couple has more time to devote to each other or to themselves, their hobbies, or careers.

For a wife the decision to have children may mean giving up her job or career plans, at least temporarily. In our culture women are still seen as the ones primarily responsible for raising children. It is not surprising then that many women pregnant with their first child report that they are planning to leave their jobs. Some are quitting until their children start school, while others are quitting permanently. Such a decision often creates financial strains since many young couples depend on two incomes. This is probably the reason why, in a recent survey by *Better Homes and Gardens*, many young women said they would remain childless until one spouse could afford to quit work and stay home with the children.

There are many reasons why couples choose to have children. Society, of course, encourages it; children are necessary for a society to continue. A couple may see their friends having children and receive not-so-subtle hints from their parents that they'd like to be grandparents. A couple may also feel unfulfilled without children: For them, being a woman and a mother, or being a husband and a father, go together. One couple explained that both of them always assumed they would have children. "My decision to marry," the wife said, "had to do with knowing that children were in our future . . . that my husband was someone to have children with." Her decision to have children, she continued, was "to experience the intense mother-child bond . . . to pass on the nurturing I had as a child." Her husband said that he wanted to know "what my child would be like; what fatherhood would be like" and he wanted to experience a father-child relationship.

During pregnancy a mother, of course, has a special involvement with the fetus growing inside her. She can experience the intense joy as well as the tremendous responsibility of feeling new life develop. Although her husband's role during pregnancy is less immediate, it is still an experience that both of them can share.

Many couples take childbirth classes together. Here they learn about the stages of labor—what is likely to happen and why. This information is especially reassuring for a wife so she can take the events of labor in her stride. The couple also learn about the techniques that a wife should follow during labor and delivery. These techniques are important for a husband to know, too, so he can coach his wife in relaxing or breathing and make the process of childbirth easier. In addition, couples learn what a newborn baby will look like and what medical procedures will be necessary for their new child.

One woman reported that her husband was "indispensable" during the hours of labor in helping her remember to practice the proper techniques. Although her husband said he was tired, he also explained how happy he was to feel needed. After the actual delivery, he was the first one to hold the baby in the delivery room. Together a mother and father and their tiny little girl shared the experience of becoming a new family.

The family cycle begins when a couple form a relationship and make a long-term commitment to each other. This commitment generally involves marriage, but an increasing number of couples are choosing to live together without getting married. For a young couple the early years of their relationship involve adjusting to new roles and responsibilities, and often learning the art of compromise and effective communication. Eventually a couple may decide to expand their family unit by having a child. This may be the most important single decision to affect a family. It changes the way that a man and woman view themselves; it changes their relationship to each other; and, for a woman especially, it often results in a totally different pattern of living.

3

THE FAMILY CYCLE CONTINUES

For a new mother the days just following the birth of her baby can be the happiest and, at the same time, the most difficult for her. The life that she carried inside her now lies cradled in her arms. With this baby goes so many of a mother's hopes and plans; so much of her love is focused on this tiny being. Yet for many women, giving birth may be followed by a mild depression known as "post partum (after birth) blues." The "blues" occur as a result of the tremendous exhaustion a woman feels after the birth experience and the change that takes place in her hormonal balance. In addition, she may experience a "letdown," quite normal following such an important event that has been nine months in preparation.

While a mother is in the hospital, she and her baby are usually the center of attention. Nurses and doctors are there to look after her and help with the child's care. The proud father generally provides support and encouragement. But eventually mother and baby must come home. Since women in our culture are still considered primarily responsible for childrearing, a mother generally finds herself alone with the baby while her husband is away at his job. Then she may experience the feelings that author Shirley Jackson describes:

Sooner or later you are going to be left alone with this baby. All alone, just you and baby and an all-pervading panic. You are reasonably sure by now that you are not going to sit down on him or put the diaper on over his head, but by golly, that is just about all you *are* sure of.

A new baby is an enormous responsibility for any woman. She may suffer great anxiety while, at the same time, feeling tremendous satisfaction from having another human being totally dependent on her. Much of her day (and night) is devoted to the baby—feeding, changing, bathing, playing, comforting. And when a mother is not actually doing for her baby, she may be worrying that the child is all right.

During this period a woman experiences the joy of participating in her child's growth. Psychologists have long realized that the first years of life are essential to an individual's future development. Many of them stress the importance of having the parents—especially the mother—present to interact with the child as much as possible at this time. Others say that it's important to have some loving, caring person nurturing the infant, but it doesn't have to be the parents, at least not all the time.

For many women the role of full-time mother is not without its difficulties. Women often say that they must try hard to keep from going "stir crazy" when they have to stay at home most of the day and their only companion is a baby. Women who gave up a career so they could be with their children may also feel resentful at no longer being in the workplace. Experts point out that there is no need for a mother to be with her child all the time. And they recommend that even an unemployed woman leave her child with a babysitter periodically so she can pursue other interests.

For a woman who must continue working, or who

chooses to continue after she has children, the demands on her can be enormous. It may be extremely difficult to find reliable child care. (In fact, some women have given up their jobs because these services were simply not available.) If a child is sick, a woman may have to take time off from work to deal with the emergency. Surveys show that when a woman works, it is she, not her husband, who still has the primary responsibility for child care as well as household chores.

Women who are successful at juggling all these responsibilities have the "best of both worlds" as one family expert puts it. These women say that the fulfillment they derive from their jobs has helped them to be better mothers.

Yet, a recent survey by *Better Homes and Gardens* shows that many women who must work, raise children, and maintain a home find it an unglamorous existence. They report not having enough time to do everything. And some of these women even said that they would enjoy having a "wife" to help them out around the house.

Perhaps, what many women would really welcome, instead of a "wife," is a little more help from their husbands. Most men, however, believe that their primary role is providing financial support for their families. Even when a wife works, the husband's paycheck is usually larger and represents the main source of income. The demands of a man's job often conflict with his spending more time at home doing chores or raising children. In addition, men have been raised to believe that it is most important for them to achieve things outside the family—on a job, or in the community. For them the achievement of being a good parent often takes second place.

Nevertheless, some men are becoming increasingly involved in the responsibilities of parenting. Psychologists point out that men are capable of providing as much nurturing as women. Men report that they find a great deal of satisfaction in spending more time teaching their children, playing with them, bathing and feeding them. Yet they are often amazed at how much time is involved in caring for children. They have also come to realize how difficult it is for women to find enough energy to handle both a job and family responsibilities.

THE GROWING FAMILY

For Herb Johnson this had been a very important day. Just an hour ago the president of the large computer company that Herb had been pitching for weeks had called to say that he wanted Herb's advertising firm to handle their new campaign. If the campaign was successful, and Herb knew it would be, it could mean a big promotion in the fall. Now, as Herb pulled his car into the driveway, he could hardly wait to tell his wife, Barbara, the news.

"Barbara, you'll never believe it . . . " Herb began as soon as he had gotten inside the kitchen door.

"Oh Herb, you're just in time," Barbara interrupted. "Would you mind feeding Mike? I just can't handle both these kids right now."

"The kids again," Herb thought resentfully. "Why can't they wait just this once?"

As Herb sat down to feed his youngest—nine-month-old Mike—Barbara launched into a lengthy description of everything the kids had done that day, from the new friend Christy had made in the neighborhood to Mike's encounter with the cat from next door.

Much later that night, after the children had been bathed and put to bed, and the house had been closed up, Herb tried once more to tell Barbara his good news. But as he turned and started talking, he noticed that she was already deep in sleep on the pillow beside him.

Inevitably children mean that a husband and wife

have far less time when they can be alone to talk and do things together. Although a father loves his children, he may feel resentful if his wife always seems to put their needs first. A woman, on the other hand, may resent the fact that her husband appears unwilling to help out more often with the children and relieve her of some of the responsibility for their care. Unless a husband and wife discuss their feelings, resentments will build, creating a wall that separates the couple and hurts their relationship.

Psychologists point out that parents should try to strike a balance in their lives. While fulfilling the responsibilities of parenting, they should also leave time for themselves and their relationship. Yet this may be more difficult in theory than in practice. Many women report feeling guilty when they put their own needs ahead of the needs of their children, as if they are failing, somehow, as mothers.

What are the important needs of children that parents should try to satisfy? One of these, of course, is love. A child who receives love, first from his parents and then from other adults, develops a strong sense of identity and self-esteem and acquires the ability to form relationships with others. As one expert put it: "To be loved provides the capacity to love. To feel rejected and unwanted is to feel skeptical of everyone."

Children need security—to know that their calls for food or for help will be answered. Security gives children the confidence to leave their families and become involved in the outside world. Parents also have to provide their children with new experiences so they can learn and develop.

Discipline refers to the rules and regulations that create order for a child. Without discipline children can feel unloved, and they will be unable to adjust to the world. Praise and punishment are a part of discipline. Children deserve praise when they abide by the rules and

*Love and security are essential
elements in a child's life.*

punishment when they break them. Children also need responsibility because this helps them become independent. As one writer explained: "Successful parents are defined in terms of their ability to rear children who can function as independent adults."

One of the most significant steps that children take toward independence occurs when they begin school, and for a growing number this step is occurring at even younger ages—3 and 4. While some tears may be shed during the first few days at school, most children seem to adjust rather quickly. A mother often welcomes the opportunity to be without her child for a few hours each day. Nevertheless, this may be the first time that the child has been outside her control, and she may worry that the youngster is not happy and secure throughout the school day.

As children grow and develop during the primary years, parents will be forced to confront many important issues regarding their upbringing. Where can children go by themselves? What can they do on their own? What should be expected of them in school? What responsibilities and privileges should they be given at home? These are only a few of the general issues that parents confront.

Here's another problem that arises in many households.

"Daddy," ten-year-old Jason began, "there's this space game I saw at the store and I asked Mommy if she'd give me an advance on my allowance so I could get it."

"What did your mother say?" his father asked.

"That I'd just have to wait till I saved the money. But, Daddy, the game might be gone by then."

"Well, Jason, I can see how much you want it. Maybe we can soften Mommy up a little," his father smiled.

"Oh, Daddy, thanks," Jason beamed. "I knew you'd help."

In Jason's family his parents often disagree over issues such as this one. Jason has learned that when his mother says "no," his father will often say "yes." Unfortunately this only teaches the boy that rules can easily be broken when you know how. It has also led to severe conflicts between Jason's parents.

Of course a husband and wife cannot be expected to agree on every issue regarding their children. But it is important for a couple to discuss these issues and try to resolve them, not only for their own relationship, but also for the healthy development of their children. A child who is confronted with a different set of rules by each parent will often feel anxious and confused or, like Jason, may attempt to play one parent off against the other.

Of course, the problems confronted by a single parent are frequently quite different. He or she carries the responsibility of raising a child almost entirely alone. Single parents often report that they miss having a spouse with whom to discuss many of the issues that arise in raising children. With a spouse a single parent could share the burden of making those important decisions that affect a child's life, as well as the necessary day-to-day tasks that are all part of childrearing.

ADOLESCENCE

I see no hope for the future of our people if they are dependent on the frivolous youth of today, for certainly all youth are reckless beyond words. . . . When I was a boy, we were taught to be discreet and respectful of elders, but the present youth are exceedingly wise and impatient of restraint.

Although this may sound like a contemporary statement, it was actually made many centuries ago by the ancient

Greek poet, Hesiod. Apparently the relationship between adolescents and adults has always been marked by conflict, criticism, and misunderstanding.

In Western culture, at least, this conflict seems inevitable. During adolescence young people experience immense physical and psychological changes that cause them to question who they are and search for a new sense of identity. In the process they come into conflict with their parents, who represent the established way of doing things. To define themselves and separate from their parents, adolescents often criticize their parents' values and rebel against their authority. Yet, at the same time, adolescents may miss the security that their parents once provided and long to be little children again. For young people this is all part of growing up and becoming fully independent individuals. Few tasks in a human being's development are more important. Unless adolescents establish a firm sense of identity apart from their parents, they will be unable to function effectively as adults or to form fulfilling relationships with other people.

In *The Diary of a Young Girl*, Anne Frank describes many of her feelings during adolescence. "I think what is happening to me is so wonderful" Anne says, "and not only what can be seen on my body, but all that is taking place inside." Anne discusses her efforts to be more independent of her family, saying that "I've drawn myself apart from them all. . . . " She also describes the conflicts with her parents and criticizes them for giving her responsibility one day and treating her as a child the next. "I'm not a baby or a spoiled darling any more, to be laughed at whatever she does. I have my own views, plans, and ideas. . . . "

As young people struggle to become more independent, their parents may feel left behind or left out. For so long they have been used to participating in many of their children's activities. Now these same young people would rather be with their friends or by themselves.

Some parents envy teenagers their independence. "He's got a lot more freedom than I had at his age," a father might say. "There was no old man to support me. I had to go to work."

Many parents are also afraid for their teenagers as they see them growing more independent. They fear that these young people may make a serious mistake and get into trouble or, worse yet, injure themselves. On the other hand, parents usually recognize that without increasing amounts of responsibility, young people will never learn how to make their own decisions and become independent adults.

So, where should the line be drawn between too much independence and not enough? This is the question that arises over and over again as parents and teenagers grapple with issues such as dating, grades, curfews, part-time jobs, or use of the family car. To deal with these issues, parents and teenagers need to show flexibility and empathy, and maintain a continuing dialogue with each other.

THE FAMILY IN MIDDLE AGE

The psychological break that young people make with their parents during adolescence has generally been followed by a physical separation as youth went off to college, went to work, and established their own households. But, at present, young people are not always leaving home quite the way they did in the past. This has occurred because of the large number of young people produced during the postwar baby boom as well as the combined effects of inflation and recession.

Today there is a high unemployment rate among young adults—higher, in fact, than the national average. There are simply too many of them and not enough of the types of jobs that they want to do or are qualified to do. As a result, many young people are often forced to remain at home and live with their parents while they, look for work. Even those fortunate enough to find jobs may not be able to afford high apartment rents, and they, too, may continue living at home.

Others, who have moved out of their parents' home and tried to make it on their own, may be forced to return. For example, if a young man becomes unemployed for a long period, he and his wife may have to move in with her parents. Or a young woman with a child may move back home after her divorce.

Two and three generations living under the same roof can create problems. Middle-aged parents may experience severe financial strain when their children and grandchildren move in with them. Everyone may feel cramped in a small house that was really designed for fewer people. Schedules may conflict, too. Young adults may disrupt their middle-aged parents' set routine by staying up late, or going out more often and returning long after their parents have gone to bed. Finally, when young adults remain at home or come back after being away, parents tend to treat them as children. One woman who moved home after her divorce explained that her mother tried to make every decision for her. This undermined the woman's authority with her own children.

Unfortunately, this complaint is expressed not only by those young adults who live with their parents, but also by millions of others who move away from home, never to return except for visits. While it is natural for parents to feel lonely when their children leave and to worry about them, some parents seem to go too far. They constantly seem to be interfering with a steady stream of advice for their children on what type of apartment to rent, what clothes to buy, what friends to have, when to settle down and get married, even what salary they ought to be paid in their jobs. Some parents are just incapable of regarding their grown children as adults.

For some women—especially those who have been

full-time mothers and homemakers—letting go of their children may be especially difficult. Their children were the primary interest of these women; their children's success meant their success as mothers. With their children gone, and the nest empty, these women may suffer from the so-called "empty-nest syndrome." They may feel that their primary role in life is over and wonder sadly what to do with themselves now.

This is not the case for the majority of women, however. Women who are employed in the workplace have another role outside their family. And even those women who are not employed may see the departure of their children as an opportunity to reenter the workplace or to do some of the other things that they didn't have time to do before.

For the middle-aged couple the children's leaving also means that they can be alone together, perhaps for the first time since they were newly married. Those couples who have maintained a fulfilling relationship over the years report that this is one of the most satisfying periods of their married lives.

Yet for a minority of couples, it is not so satisfying. Parents may sit across the table from each other and realize that they have little in common now that the children are gone. For years the children had been their major focus of attention, and maybe even their only topic of conversation. Over a period of time a mother and father may have forgotten how to relate to each other as a husband and wife, the way they once did before the children came.

While the couple is going through a crisis in their marriage, each one may also be going through a period of personal reevaluation. Adults have now entered the last half of their lives, and they often fear that time is running out for them. A man may look back at his life and feel that he hasn't achieved the career goals he set for himself. Or he may feel that his marriage is no longer satisfying. So he decides to get a divorce and find someone else.

A woman may look in the mirror and see the tiny wrinkles that tell her she is getting older. In a culture that idolizes youth, it is easy for her to feel that the best years are behind her. During middle age women also go through menopause, when their monthly periods stop, and they are no longer able to bear children. For a few women, at least, menopause is a further indication that they are not useful anymore, although most women pass through this period without undue stress.

For the vast majority of people, middle age brings its own satisfactions and rewards. It is often a time when a couple is freed from the responsibilities of raising children to take on a greater role in their community. It can be a time when a man or woman finally achieves a top-level job, with the status and high pay that go with it. Finally, for a married couple mid-life is often a time when they find renewed fulfillment in their relationship.

THE LAST PHASE—OLD AGE

The poet Robert Browning wrote:

Grow old along with me!
The best is yet to be,
the last of life for which
the first was made. . . .

For a married couple old age is the final phase of the family life cycle. It begins with retirement and continues until the death of one of the spouses.

Some people look forward to retirement, but for others it is a difficult adjustment. The man or woman whose identity is his or her job may feel especially useless with no work to go to every day. The only way to avoid this problem is to develop interests outside of a job. A hobby or volunteer activity, for example, can often be pursued for a lifetime.

Millions of older people find great satisfaction in their role as grandparents. Since a grandparent is not directly responsible for the upbringing of a grandchild, their relationship can be far more relaxed and carefree than that between a parent and child.

Besides retirement there are many other adjustments that a couple must make in old age. First, they must adjust to living on less income. It is true that the financial needs of the elderly may be less, since they no longer go to work, their home mortgages are often paid off, and their social security benefits are generally tax free. Nevertheless, their medical expenses are often extremely high, and are not all covered by Medicare or Medicaid.

Out of a total population of about 26 million elderly citizens, 15 percent live below the poverty line, and many others live just above it. The sunset years are frequently not as golden as they are portrayed.

A second type of adjustment for retired couples is to a different pattern of living. For the first time, married couples are at home together every day, and this can create friction. Many people, however, seem to adjust to this new routine, for national surveys indicate that marriage relationships for the majority of old people are very satisfying. While many stress the companionship their marriage brings, some also report enjoying sexual relations well into their later years.

A third type of adjustment for old people is to the loss of the familiar. Friends die, neighborhoods change, grown children move out of town and across the country. But, by far the most difficult adjustment is to failing health, especially as people become quite elderly. Eyesight and hearing decline; bones become brittle and break more easily; muscles lose their strength. With declining health may go a loss of independence. Generally it is the husband whose health goes first because the normal lifespan is shorter for men than for women. At the beginning, his wife may be able to care for him. But

*Age brings the joys
of being a grandparent.*

as his condition worsens, she may have to put him in a hospital or convalescent home. And eventually death takes him.

The family cycle is now complete, at least for one family. It began with the relationship of two adults and continued through the birth of their children, childrearing, the departure of the children from home, the middle age of the parents, and finally their old age. But the family cycle does not end here. It continues to turn for all the generations to come.

4

MAKING FAMILIES WORK

There is probably no one who passes smoothly through every stage of the family cycle. Along the way all of us must solve problems or deal with crises. Experts point out that the amount of satisfaction couples report in their marriage declines soon after they take their vows. This is probably due to the unrealistic expectations of many couples that marriage will consist mainly of candlelight and romantic moments in front of the fire. The decline in satisfaction seems to continue through the birth of a couple's children and until the youngsters have started school. During the remainder of the family cycle, three different trends may take place. For some couples there is a further decline in their relationship; for others a leveling off occurs; and still others experience an improvement in their relationship.

Many couples seem destined to discover that marriage involves more problems than they anticipated. The question is how many of these problems could have been prevented or solved. Many married couples seem to believe that a marriage simply runs along on its own. A husband and wife may drift apart slowly, almost unaware of it. Or, if they are aware, feel that little can be done about it. They may even envy other couples who have a more satisfying relationship and wish that theirs had turned out better.

A fulfilling marriage doesn't just happen. It takes time and work. It takes the same commitment that we make to our jobs . . . to our children . . . to ourselves.

This is not to say that a couple should ever expect to achieve perfect harmony. Disagreements and conflicts are natural whenever two people live together. In fact, it is far better for a couple to get their disagreements out in the open than to keep them inside where they will often fester and grow worse. But it is also important for a husband and wife to work out their conflicts in a constructive way.

Constructive conflict management means that a couple need to state their grievances without feeling under attack and without trying to tear each other down. They must be assured that each one is really listening to the other. They should be willing to give feedback to show that whatever was said has been understood. Finally, each partner should state what he or she wants the other to do and try to find a solution that is agreeable to both of them.

Here's an example:

Wife: "I wish you hadn't bought that new TV."

Husband: "You never like me to enjoy myself, do you?"

(This is not what the man's wife said. Such a general statement, which indicates that he feels attacked, might prevent the man's wife from saying anything further and the conflict would never get resolved.)

Husband might have said: "Why didn't you want me to get this TV just now?"

(This type of feedback shows he was listening.)

Wife: "The old one is perfectly good enough. And there are some other things we need much more."

Husband: "What do you want me to do?"

Wife: "I don't know. I just wish we could get along the way we did when we were still going out together."

(This type of response is much too vague. The wife doesn't really tell her husband what she wants him to do.)

Wife might have said: "I'd like to talk about these big purchases first and agree on them before you go ahead."

Of course, a couple may not be able to work out all their conflicts. But many can be resolved if a husband and wife use the techniques of constructive conflict management. In the rest of this chapter, we will look at some of the issues that create conflicts in a family and suggest possible solutions.

MONEY

"My husband never takes any responsibility. The only way the bills get paid is for me to pay them."

"Every time I make up a budget for this family, my wife goes out and buys some expensive toys for the kids or a big present for her mother. She just doesn't care whether we go to the poor house."

"If my husband really loved me, he'd buy me that new car I want."

"Steven is a credit card freak. He gets every card he can and charges them to the limit. It really frightens me, but I can't make him stop."

"We never have enough money. I wish my husband earned more so we could afford to send the kids to camp like everybody else in our neighborhood."

Money is a constant source of complaint among many husbands and wives. Perhaps it's because money seems so important and represents such important things—

Managing the family's finances responsibly
is a good way to
avoid conflicts in a marriage.

such as love, security, power, status, independence—to people. For example, the woman who wants her husband to buy her that new car obviously equates money with love. And the man who complains that his wife is always buying some expensive toys probably believes that their financial security is flying out the window.

One way for couples to avoid conflicts involving money is to sit down and discuss how their money should be spent. Many couples put together a budget that includes fixed expenses, such as rent and utilities, and discretionary expenses, such as clothing and recreation. A budget gives a couple a realistic look at what they can and cannot spend, based on their income. Of course, each spouse must then take responsibility for staying within the budget and agree to talk about any unusual expenditures (such as the new TV in the earlier example).

A responsible approach to handling money is extremely important, should a couple have a low income and have trouble making ends meet. Today millions of Americans—young, middle aged, and elderly—live at or below the poverty level, and for them life is a constant struggle.

Even for more affluent couples, a severe problem arises should a spouse become unemployed. This especially holds when a husband is the sole support of his family. Any huge debts that a couple may have run up needlessly can prove devastating. And a couple who has neglected to put any money aside can find themselves in serious financial trouble almost immediately.

This situation is further complicated by the fact that so much of a man's identity and sense of self-worth come from his job and his success as a provider. The nonworking wife may also feel that her status and prestige are directly tied to her husband's job and the amount of money he earns.

Today, however, the majority of families in America

are two-income families. Even if a husband becomes unemployed, his wife continues earning an income (although it may only be from a part-time job). While this has helped many families get through recent recessions, it may have left some husbands with very bruised egos because they found themselves feeling totally dependent on their wives.

SEXUAL PROBLEMS

Sexual dissatisfaction is one of the complaints heard most often among married couples. In a *Ladies Home Journal* survey, one-third of the women responding mentioned "a lack of interest or pleasure in sex." A *McCalls* survey showed that although many women had found emotional fulfillment in their marriages, only 37 percent had found "sexual fulfillment." Women complain about the quality as well as the frequency of sexual relations. Men complain about the same things.

Experts are quick to point out that if a couple is having an unsatisfying sexual relationship, it may reflect the fact that their entire relationship has become unsatisfying, boring, and routine. A married couple who refer to each other as "Mom" and "Dad," for instance, may be unable to regard each other any longer as lovers. Perhaps they have grown accustomed to focusing on other concerns besides their relationship. A woman may devote herself to her children; and a man may spend fifteen hours a day on his job. Each has little time, energy, or interest left for the other.

If a couple want to make their relationship more satisfying, this has to become their top priority. It's amazing what two people can do once they make the decision to do it. But this is not always easy. A couple may have to get reacquainted almost as they did when they dated or during their engagement period. As the marriage relationship begins to improve, a couple's sexual relationship often improves, too. Spouses must learn to understand their own sexual desires and communicate effectively about what they enjoy in a sexual relationship. And they should be realistic about their partner's ability to fulfill these desires.

LEISURE TIME

Planning a weekend outing or a vacation can easily turn into a family argument where everyone ends up dissatisfied. For instance, with summer vacation a month away, the children may want to go to the lake; their mother may have her heart set on a trip to the mountains; and her husband may want to take a sightseeing tour along the West Coast. Since all of these things are not possible in a single week, the family must discuss the alternatives and be willing to compromise.

In some families one person may end up in charge of planning vacations. Frequently, though, that person resents taking on the entire responsibility. And the other family members may resent this situation, too, because they are often forced to go somewhere they don't want to go. Only by discussing this problem, recognizing everyone's feelings, and sharing the responsibility for vacations can they become a more satisfying experience.

Each week, family members also need leisure time available to them and the chance to use it as creatively as possible. This usually requires a willingness on the part of parents and children to work together. For instance, a woman may want to take evening courses at a local college. This means that her husband will have to pitch in and cook dinner for their children on those nights. Or a couple may want to go out one evening each week to the movies, which means that their teenage son will have to babysit his younger siblings. If parents and children are willing to help each other, then many of their needs can be met successfully.

PARENTS AND IN-LAWS

Parents and in-laws represent an age-old problem for married couples—one that many couples are never able to deal with successfully.

Stan grew up in a family where his mother and father maintained a polite but distant relationship. Stan's father owned a hardware store and spent seven days a week running the business. His mother, feeling lonely and abandoned, came to rely more and more on Stan. She would talk to Stan about the frustrations of her marriage, ask his advice before she made any decisions, and share her secrets with him. Stan had almost taken on the role of a husband to his mother—a role he seemed willing to play because he felt sorry for his mother and hated the way his father treated her.

When the time came for Stan to marry, a crisis occurred in the family. Stan's mother had always said: "I will love any woman you choose." But, in fact, she deeply resented Stan's fiancée for taking her son away and treated her very badly.

After Stan was married, his mother continued calling him for advice all the time and expected that she could come over to his house whenever she needed him. Stan's wife felt this was a needless intrusion on their lives and wanted him to tell his mother to stop.

Stan felt caught between both the women in his life. He tried to please each of them, but ended up satisfying neither one.

The close bonds that unite a parent and child can easily create difficulties in a marriage. As in Stan's case, a son may be unwilling to tell his mother that she can no longer depend on him so heavily. A woman may find herself in a similar situation. Or she may be like a little girl—extremely dependent on her mother and father, and unwilling to do anything without their approval. If her husband happens to disagree with what she and her parents want to do, he may find himself in a very uncomfortable situation.

Family life experts point out that the woman who remains her parents' "little girl" or the man who remains a "Mamma's boy" cannot have a satisfying marriage relationship. Individuals must separate themselves from their parents, develop their own identities, and establish their independence. Only then can they create a meaningful relationship with a marriage partner.

This does not mean, of course, that a young married couple should forget about their parents. Even after they are married, a husband continues to be a son and a wife continues to be a daughter; and each takes on the added role of son-in-law and daughter-in-law. Interactions between in-laws can be rewarding for everyone, although some conflicts are bound to occur. For example, a young mother may not raise her children to the complete satisfaction of her mother-in-law. But these kinds of issues need not create conflicts, if mother-in-law and daughter-in-law remain flexible.

As a married couple grows older, they often have to take on greater responsibility for an aged parent or parent-in-law. Now the roles of parent and child may be reversed. And it may be difficult for husbands and wives, who once relied on their parents, to see them now becoming weak and dependent. In some cases a couple might decide to take an elderly parent into their home, which can create a tense situation. The elderly person may resent losing his or her independence and feel uncomfortable in someone else's household. A nonworking wife may be forced to take over the entire task of caring for this individual, which may be especially trying if it is her mother-in-law or father-in-law. A couple and their growing children may also feel a loss of privacy with another person in the household.

An ongoing discussion of all these issues is essential if three generations are to live together satisfactorily. A husband and wife must be willing to share responsibility for taking care of an elderly person. Children, parents, and grandparents must also be willing to compromise so they can still do the things they want and get along with each other.

Some couples, of course, ultimately decide to place an elderly parent in a nursing home. They may be unable—and perhaps unwilling—to adequately care for the aged person at home, especially if he or she suffers from extremely poor health. For most couples, however, this course of action is just as difficult—if not more so—than caring for the aged parent themselves. Couples often experience guilt and feel they are abandoning their parent, even though the nursing home care they obtain may be the very best.

PARENTS AND CHILDREN

Many family conflicts involve children and the way they are to be raised. Since there is not space in this book to describe all of them, only one has been selected as an example: discipline.

Mother: "My husband is too strict with our children. He demands far too much of them."

Father: "I think my wife is far too easy with the kids. She lets them get away with everything. If you don't expect a lot from kids, and let them know you expect it, they won't do anything."

Parents frequently disagree over how much discipline is healthy for their children and what to do when a child disobeys. Some parents seem to lose sight of the fact that discipline is designed to benefit their children and set necessary limits for them. Instead it may become part of a continuing battle between the parents themselves. For example, a woman may decide that her little boy will not be allowed to watch an extra half hour of TV, although her husband thinks it's all right. The half

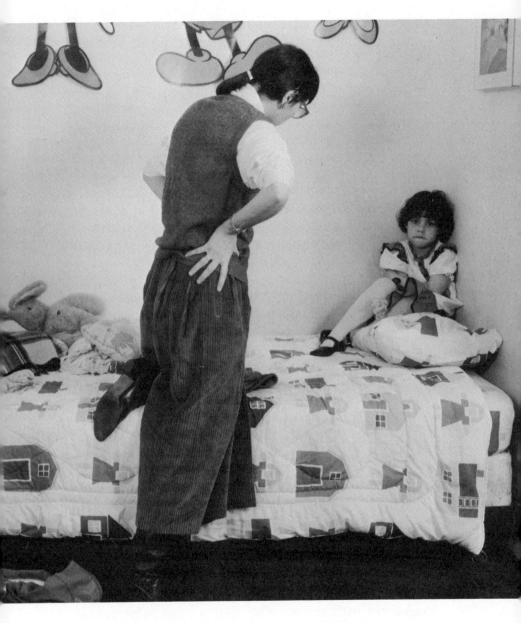

Disciplining children can be a source
of disagreement between husband and wife.

hour of TV and its effect on the child may be less important to the mother than winning an argument with her
husband. She wants to assert her dominance and this is
one way to do it.

Conflicts over discipline also erupt between parents
and children. It is natural for children to test the limits
that their parents set for them; and this testing process
usually increases as children reach adolescence. While
young people feel capable of handling more freedom,
their parents may fear that they are not yet mature
enough.

Some of these conflicts can be avoided if parents and
children can remember whom discipline is designed to
help and what it is supposed to accomplish. In some families discipline is always imposed by the parents. But in
other families, as children grow older, they take part in
deciding what their responsibilities will be and what limits will be imposed on their activities. Thus, discipline
becomes a family issue that everyone deals with
together.

SEEKING HELP

Sometimes a family may be unable to solve its problems
alone. In these situations family members can seek outside, professional help from a counselor or therapist.
Today there are more than 10,000 members of the American Association for Marriage and Family Therapy. They
include psychologists, social workers, clergy, and others
who have been specially trained to help with family
problems.

Many people, however, are reluctant to seek the help
of a counselor. They feel that they should be able to solve
their own problems, and they are often unwilling to discuss them with anyone else. Yet, if these same people
were suffering from a serious physical illness, they would
not try to treat it themselves but would immediately go

to a doctor. When a marriage or family relationship is seriously ill, it too requires the services of a trained professional.

Even if people decide to enter counseling, they may still have very unrealistic notions of what its purpose is. One spouse, for example, may agree to counseling because he or she expects the counselor to agree that the other spouse is the cause of all the conflicts in their marriage and blame that spouse for everything. But a counselor's role is not to fix blame. It is to give a married couple or an entire family a chance to air their grievances.

The counselor's office also serves as a place where family members may be able to discuss their problems more readily than in the highly charged atmosphere at home.

Counselors try to facilitate these discussions. For example, a major source of friction in a family may be a teenage son's performance in school. Although his intelligence is well above average, the teenager may be doing very poorly. Family counseling reveals that the teenager's father belittles academic learning. He resents his son's intelligence and feels threatened by it. As a result, the boy performs far below his capabilities, although this angers his mother and creates a conflict between them. She may also feel angry toward her husband for his treatment of the boy as well as for other reasons.

Family counseling can provide a useful perspective on problems such as these and help family members find solutions. But these solutions often take time. And some problems—whether between parents and children, or husband and wife—may prove entirely unsolvable.

5

SEPARATION AND DIVORCE

For many families who are unable to solve their problems, the family life cycle is broken by separation and divorce. Throughout this century the number of divorces has been rising steadily, and presently there are more than 1 million divorces each year—more than triple the total in 1960. This means that for every two marriages, there is one divorce. In a recent poll the majority of Americans believe that most couples getting married today don't expect to remain married to each other for the rest of their lives. This does not suggest that marriage itself is going out of style. The overwhelming number of people who divorce marry again; and some of them marry twice, three times, or even more often.

WHY IS THE DIVORCE RATE SO HIGH?

Experts believe that the high divorce rate has been caused by a combination of factors. In the past the institution of marriage seemed more important than the individual husband or wife. To keep their families together, wives and husbands were prepared to sacrifice their own happiness; and many probably did. Today individuals are far less willing to engage in self-sacrifice and far more concerned with their own personal happiness. In fact, the major function of marriage and the family, as far as most people are concerned, is to provide each member with personal fulfillment. If a marriage is not doing this, and is actually making the partners unhappy, most husbands and wives feel free to leave and try again with someone else. Commenting on the American desire to have complete freedom of choice, Margaret Mead once wrote:

> The emphasis on choice carried to its final limits means in marriage, as it does at every other point in American life, that no choice is irrevocable. All persons should be allowed to move if they don't like their present home, change schools, change friends, change political parties, change religious affiliations. . . . Why should marriage be the exception?

A second factor affecting the divorce rate has been the changing status of women. In years past many women felt forced to remain in unhappy marriages because they couldn't support themselves. This is no longer true. A majority of wives work at paying jobs, and even those who don't can generally find paid employment if they decide to get divorced. In addition, divorced women can start businesses, obtain credit, and own their own homes. These rights were usually denied women, and especially divorced women, until the last few years when changes occurred, largely in response to pressure from the Women's Movement.

Divorce—like many other social customs—seems to have a snowball effect. As more people get divorced, it becomes acceptable for others to follow. In fact, all of us probably know someone—a friend or relative—who has recently experienced a divorce in their family. Our standards of morality have changed. The divorced person is no longer looked down on as someone who is immoral . . . a social outcast. Most of the churches have also relaxed their attitudes regarding divorce, making the decision easier for many of their members.

But, it is the state legislatures that have done the most to ease the divorce process by passing very liberal divorce laws. In the past, for a court to grant a divorce, one spouse had to be proven guilty of some grievous offense such as adultery. Now most states have no-fault divorce. Instead of one spouse being at fault, both spouses can simply claim that their differences cannot be overcome, and a divorce will be granted.

So far, we have looked at those factors that have created an atmosphere in which divorce is acceptable and rather easy to obtain. But what actually causes an individual couple to seek a divorce? In some cases one spouse may suffer from a severe problem such as alcoholism or compulsive gambling. After years of trying to deal with this illness and seeing it get no better, the other spouse may finally call it quits.

More often, though, divorce occurs as a result of a combination of problems like those we discussed in the preceding chapter. These may include sexual incompatibility; in-law problems; an inability to handle money; or infidelity.

For some time Joan had felt neglected by her husband. Larry was a young account executive at an advertising agency who left for work every morning at 7:00 A.M. and rarely arrived home before 9 o'clock at night. When Joan tried to talk to her husband, he would just shrug. "I'm doing it for you and the girls," he'd say. "The agency's not going to promote me and pay me a big salary unless I'm willing to work for it."

Gradually Joan and Larry grew farther apart. And whenever they were together, an argument always seemed to break out between them. At the agency Larry was assigned a big project that involved his working closely with a female colleague. Eventually they drifted into an affair. One day when Joan was cleaning out the pockets in Larry's suits to take them to the cleaners, she found a note that revealed the entire relationship. That night Joan confronted her husband and demanded a divorce.

Sometimes a single incident—such as discovering an affair—can be the final straw that breaks a marriage. By that time a couple may have gone through a long period of open conflict. A husband may criticize his wife for neglecting their children because of her job, for being a poor cook or a sloppy housekeeper. She may be just as critical of him for the way he dresses, the small salary he earns, or the bowling buddies he goes out with every weekend. These conflicts may not be confined to the privacy of a couple's home, but spill over into social occasions. A wife, for instance, may criticize her husband at a cocktail party in front of their friends. He naturally feels hurt and embarrassed that his wife would treat him this way. But she may just be getting back at him for something he said earlier while they were still at home dressing for the party.

As the conflicts continue, the hurt grows deeper. And both spouses feel their self-esteem is being destroyed. Eventually one spouse might decide to leave; but the first separation might not be permanent. The spouse returns and there is a reconciliation that could last days or weeks. But more conflicts follow, and eventually one spouse leaves permanently.

Of course, all marriage breakdowns do not follow the same pattern. For some couples there may be few open conflicts; they may simply keep the hurt and anger inside. Yet the hostility is just as great. Both spouses may be unable to share anything except perhaps the love they have for their children. In fact, as parents, both spouses may function very effectively although as husband and wife they no longer relate at all. Then, one day, the husband may come home and announce that he's "had it" and wants a divorce. And his wife may be taken completely by surprise.

A PAINFUL DECISION

For many people the decision to separate and divorce is very painful, and one they only make reluctantly. Regardless of how unhappy their marriages have been, the other person has been an important part of their lives—often for many years—and they are unwilling to end the relationship. That old saying "I can't live with you and I can't live without you" is enough to keep many destructive marriages going long after they should have ended.

A majority of people are also fearful of being alone or trying to find someone with whom to begin a new relationship. They may panic at the very idea of getting along on their own and doing everything for themselves. Other couples may also stay together because they don't want to give up all the material possessions—houses, cars, etc.—that they've accumulated over the years.

Many parents fear the effects of a divorce on their children. It may be true that two parents are better than one—that is, if they create a warm, loving environment for their children. But, if two parents are unhappy and fighting all the time, their children may be far better off with one of them gone.

Nevertheless, a divorce generally brings changes in a family's financial situation. A man whose entire income went to support one home suddenly must support two. This will frequently mean that he can provide fewer material things for his children. In addition, a woman who was a full-time homemaker before the divorce will usually have to go out to work and, as a result, will have less time to spend with her children. These considera-

*The decision to end a
marriage is never an easy one.*

tions may weigh heavily on parents as they decide to separate and divorce.

Once the separation occurs, a couple often experience a very painful period of readjustment. Whenever we form strong attachments to people, it is difficult to separate from them. As small children, the experience of being separated from our parents was very hard. This experience is repeated when we separate from a spouse.

One man described the experience as a "sick, hollow feeling in the pit of my stomach. My wife and I knew the marriage wasn't working. We tried marriage counseling, but that didn't seem to do any good. Finally, we decided to separate. It was awful! We were like little children when one of them moves away and the other is left behind."

Spouses generally continue to think about each other long after the separation, and for a time, they may be unable to concentrate on anything else. One person reported being in a "daze, or a fog, as if nothing was real." Even if friends have been divorced, as is usually the case, you're never really prepared when the same thing happens to you. Frequently the tendency is to look back on the marriage, remembering the good times and forgetting many of the bad ones. Many people regret their decision and some even decide to go back and try again.

For the rest, a sense of euphoria at having a chance to start over again seems to alternate with feelings of depression. It's like being on a roller-coaster—up one day and down the next. Guilt is another feeling often experienced by spouses who initiate a divorce because it is easy for them to believe that they have abandoned their families. A husband or wife who remains behind may, in turn, feel rejected.

Although spouses may try to maintain friendly relations during their separation, this is often impossible.

When two people have maintained a close, intimate relationship for any period of time, breaking up frequently leads to hurt feelings, pain, and conflict.

Generally each spouse retains an attorney—or both spouses may use the same attorney—who draws up an agreement that spells out the terms of a legal separation. [This must be approved by the court and later will be incorporated in the divorce decree that legally ends the marriage.] The separation agreement focuses on three broad areas: property division, alimony (financial support for a spouse), child custody and child support. These can create bitter conflicts between a husband and wife and bad feelings on both sides.

Let's say a husband, for example, agrees to give his wife their house and continue making mortgage payments on it. Inside, he may angrily resent having to do this, feeling that he has been stripped of something that he worked hard to acquire. Alimony payments often become a bloody battleground between spouses. A husband may claim that he cannot afford to pay what his wife feels she is entitled to receive. Some husbands may make alimony payments for awhile, then stop, or send the payments late, creating severe financial problems for their families. A similar situation may arise with child support.

Today the courts usually grant custody of the children to the mother. Yet in an increasing number of cases, fathers have been granted custody. Some parents share custody, and children may spend part of the week with their father and the rest with their mother. When one parent recieves custody, the other is usually granted visitation rights to see the children and take them for certain periods throughout the year. While some parents handle custody and visitation very successfully, for others it becomes just another cause of conflict. We will look at this more closely in the following chapter.

DIVORCE AND CHILDREN

This year, approximately one million children will experience the breakup of their families through separation and divorce. Perhaps they will first learn about it the way thirteen-year-old Karen did. Karen's parents sat down with her one evening and explained that they could no longer live together. Yet they reassured Karen that both of them loved her very much and would always be available whenever she needed them. Or perhaps they will find out the way ten-year-old Shawn and his younger sister Sally did. They came home from school one afternoon to find their mother in the living room, crying. And she told them that their father had left, for good.

Regardless of how much conflict has occurred between two parents, very few children seem relieved when one of them decides to leave. Instead, children generally have a very adverse reaction, and all the reassurance in the world does little to change it. When children first learn that their parents are splitting up, they may get extremely angry and blame their parents for destroying the family. Karen began to cry and tearfully asked her parents to reconsider even though she realized that they might be better off living apart. Some children show little or no emotion and say nothing. The shock of their parents' divorce seems to have numbed their feelings.

During the initial stages of a separation, children need their parents the most. But it is just at this time that parents are too preoccupied with their own problems to give children enough attention. Shawn's mother, for example, was in a state of shock for days after her husband left. And when she finally did come out of it, she had to begin looking for a full-time job to help support herself and her children. Karen's mother was more fortunate. She was better prepared to cope with the divorce, and she had also been working full-time since Karen started school. But Karen desperately missed her father. Of course, he made visits on a regular basis, but it was just not the same as having him at home where Karen could talk to him whenever she wanted.

Studies have shown that, during the first months of a family breakup, there are some broad similarities in the way all children react as well as some major differences between children in various age groups. When a parent departs, the world of the young, preschool child is severly shaken. Children often fear that the other parent will go too, leaving them completely abandoned. Young children yearn for the return of the absent parent and hope that somehow Mom and Dad will be magically reunited and everything will be the way it was before.

At the same time, children may feel rejected by the parent who departed. A mother who often says "Your father rejected me for another woman" simply reinforces these feelings. Many children worry that the parent who remains may not be able to cope with the situation, especially if they see their father or mother looking sad and depressed most of the time. As children grow older, they often worry that the remaining parent won't be able to support them financially. They imagine a refrigerator with no food in it, or no new clothes to wear to school. Sadly, for some children, these fears become all too real.

Young children commonly harbor feelings of guilt regarding the divorce, as if somehow they were the cause of it. A little girl may remember the times she disobeyed her father and he got angry and punished her. She may feel that this was the reason why he left; and the next time she sees him, the little girl will promise to always be good if her father will only come home.

Among older children—between ages 6 and 12— guilt feelings are far less common. Yet these children commonly share with their younger brothers and sisters a deep sadness when a parent departs, as well as an intense loneliness. When you've been used to having two parents to give you love and attention, one is simply not enough, especially when that parent is apt to be preoccupied with other things.

In many broken families children find themselves in the midst of a bitter conflict—torn between a mother and father whose love has turned to hate, and eventually forced to take sides.

Rachel and Carl had divorced after ten years of marriage. Rachel wanted to pursue a singing career and, when Carl objected, she left him and their two children. Carl was extremely bitter and gradually began to turn the children against her. At first, ten-year-old John seemed to resist. He loved his mother and looked forward to her visits, even if they were infrequent. But finally Carl won him over. John no longer tried to defend what his mother had done and refused to see her when she came to visit.

Adolescents usually understand, much better than younger children, why their parents divorce; nevertheless, they often have many of the same reactions. Although adolescents are moving toward independence, they still look to their families for safety and security. Divorce removes the family as a safe harbor and often pushes young people to become independent before they are ready. It is quite common for adolescents to feel abandoned by their parents and angry at them for breaking up the family. At a time when adolescents still look to their parents for advice and guidance, it is easy to believe that parents are just too busy with their own lives to care.

A parent may make a change in life style, start wearing different clothes, and begin dating again. Just when a young person needs an adult to lean on, his or her parents may start acting like adolescents. In some families there is a complete role reversal, and parents begin relying on their adolescent children for advice and support.

Many young people rise to the occasion and try to help their parents as much as possible with everything from dating to managing the household. But inside, a young person may still feel resentful and ask, "Why me?"

METHODS OF COPING

While coping with your parents' divorce is never easy, there are a few things to keep in mind that may help you get through it. First, be aware of your feelings regarding the divorce. Too many people try to act as if nothing is happening, as if they and their families are not experiencing a major crisis in their lives. But if you don't deal with your feelings now and work through them, they can create real problems for you later on.

It's natural to have feelings of anger, hurt, fear, rejection, and sadness. At times these feelings may overwhelm you and make it impossible to concentrate on anything else. Little things may irritate you more than usual. And you may find yourself getting angry for almost no reason, at your friends, your parents, or your brothers and sisters. These reactions are common during a divorce. Frequently it helps to share your feelings with someone else—someone who has gone through the same experience.

Some people also enjoy spending time with friends whose families are close, loving, and together. This can provide the type of warm, supportive environment that your family can't give you, at least at the moment. But, be careful! This type of situation might remind you of all the things that are currently lacking in your family and only intensify all the feelings you have about the divorce.

One way to take your mind off these feelings is extracurricular activities. Sports, for example, can help you work out your anger. If you're feeling rejected by your parents or hurt by them, doing well in sports or another activity can restore your self-confidence and make you feel a lot better. Learning a new skill can help, too. It's important to realize that there's very little you can do about your parents' decision to divorce, but there's plenty you can do about the way you cope with it.

One girl kept a diary where she recorded her thoughts and feelings.

> It's Saturday—I'm feeling lonely because my Dad used to be home on Saturdays and we'd go into town together and have lunch sometimes. But he just got a new apartment down state so I don't see him so much anymore. Susan's supposed to come over in about an hour. Her parents are taking us to the crafts fair. I'd really rather be going with my own Mom and Dad. But I'm sure I'll have a pretty good time just the same.

THE SINGLE-PARENT FAMILY

Today, there are approximately 12.5 million children under the age of 18 who live in single-parent families. The vast majority of these families have been created as a result of separation and divorce. And most of them— as many as 90 percent—are headed by women.*

In the preceding chapter we looked at the divorce process. Now we will look at the aftermath of divorce and how it affects the people involved, by examining the single-parent family—its parent and children—as well as the role of the visiting parent. We will be focusing on single-parent families headed by women, since this is the most typical situation.

COPING WITH CHANGE

The separated or divorced person is forced to cope with a variety of changes. Not the least of these is a change in

---

*Since 1970 the number of children living in single-parent families has nearly doubled. This is due not only to the increase in divorce, but also to the number of single women having children.

identity. No longer are you a husband or a wife. Now you're single again; and if you've been married for many years, this can really take some getting used to.

For the woman whose identity has been as a mother and helpmate to her husband, being suddenly single can be especially difficult. A woman may have depended on her husband's position in the business or professional world to give her status, prestige, and financial security. She was "Mrs. so-and-so" and proud of it!

Now all this is gone. And a woman who hadn't seen herself as a separate person or thought very much about her own identity—apart from being her husband's wife—may be left asking: "Who am I?" It can be at once a frightening, as well as exhilarating, question. And finding the answers takes struggle, experimentation, and the willingness to make a number of mistakes along the way. For some women, their journey on the road toward self-realization takes months, if not years, and it often gets extremely bumpy.

Most women are immediately faced with a tremendous change in their financial circumstances. When a spouse departs, there may be one less person in the family, but expenses—rent, utilities, food, clothing—remain almost the same. So, even if a former husband is giving over half his income as child support and alimony, it won't be enough when his family had needed the entire income to live on in the past. Of course, many women aren't awarded anywhere near this much alimony or child support. And even those that are can't always count on receiving it. A large number of husbands fail to make their alimony and child support payments.

Consequently 75 percent of divorced women work. While money is the primary motive, there are psychological reasons too. The woman who had been a full-time homemaker may find that her job is no longer rewarding because her husband isn't there any more to appreciate it. She had carried out her responsibilities as one-half of a partnership; now that the partnership is broken, these tasks no longer seem so important, nor do they yield much satisfaction.

In contrast, a paying job can give a woman a greater feeling of self-esteem and a sense of accomplishment. The company of coworkers can also help overcome the loneliness that afflicts many divorced women. Without a spouse around any longer, the friendship of other adults becomes more important than ever. Finally, many women who must stay home and care for young children complain of "cabin fever" from being confined so much. A job provides a welcome relief and an outlet.

But as a relief from the children, a job can be a double-edged sword. Many single mothers report feeling guilty when they have to leave their children and go to work. And some mothers have even decided to go on welfare rather than take jobs so they could remain at home, especially if their children are preschoolers. Part-time jobs, of course, allow mothers greater flexibility and permit them to spend more time with their children. But the pay is generally low in these positions; nor do they come with any important benefits such as medical insurance. Some women are in a real bind. They want to work—at least part time—and be self-sufficient. But, if they take a job, they risk losing the medical coverage for their children that welfare provides. A few women—freelance writers for example—have work they can do at home, but the vast majority of single mothers are not so fortunate.

For mothers who leave home to go to work, finding adequate child care can be extremely difficult. Some are fortunate enough to live near their parents, who seem only too happy to help out whenever they can. But grandparents generally aren't available every day. And they frequently have their own ideas about the best way of bringing up children, which can lead to conflicts.

Some single parents rely on babysitters. They may

drop their children off with the sitter every morning, or the sitter may come to them. While this type of care is often adequate, the child is rarely provided with any kind of enrichment experiences throughout the day.

Many single parents prefer a good day-care center where their children can be with peers and have an opportunity to develop social, as well as intellectual, skills. But these centers are usually hard to find and just as frequently quite expensive. As one expert put it: "The system simply fails many people. There is insufficient care for low-income families, there are middle-income families who have trouble paying the full cost of care, and there is a shortage of quality centers at any price."

In addition, single parents are often uncomfortable putting their children in centers all day. They feel that two-, three-, and four-year-olds are too young to be spending such long days in a "school-like" atmosphere and are better off spending at least part of the day at home. Although these women may have little choice but to use day care, they may feel guilty for doing so. Most research, however, shows that day-care centers are not bad for children. They are a mixed blessing, just like any child-care arrangement, including Mom's staying at home.

For most single parents life is nothing short of hectic. One woman began her day at 6:15 A.M. She got her children up from bed, dressed them, and prepared their breakfast. Then she got herself ready for work. There was usually no time to do the dishes, so she just left them in the sink. On the way to her office she dropped her older daughter at school and left her younger daughter with a sitter. Sometimes the woman was able to get home at lunch and put a stew or casserole on the stove for dinner. But usually she stopped at the market after work to do some shopping; picked up her younger daughter from the sitter; and arrived home about 5:00. Then she prepared the evening meal. After everything was cleaned up, the family might spend an hour watching television, or the woman might read to her younger daughter, or help her older girl with homework. Both children were usually in bed by 9:00 P.M. Then the woman did a little house cleaning and laundry and ironed something to wear for the next day. If she was lucky, there might be an hour left at the end of the day for her to call her own.

Studies have shown that eighteen months after a divorce many women report feeling somewhat overwhelmed by all the tasks that confront them. It's like having two full-time jobs. While in most marriages a working wife is also primarily responsible for housekeeping and child care, at least her husband is there to help out if necessary. He can share some of the responsibilities of raising children, and he may have taken care of outside work around the house, such as lawn mowing. But, most importantly, he is there to talk to and consult when decisions have to be made.

The single parent must do all these things alone.

PARENTS AND CHILDREN

Children in a single-parent family usually have different roles and responsibilities than their friends in two-parent families. With only one parent, and that parent generally working at a job full-time, children are naturally expected to do more to help out at home. If all the household chores are ever to get done, everyone has to pitch in with cleaning, cooking, shopping, laundry, and handling babysitting chores. Some children may harbor mixed feelings about this situation.

Lisa envied many of her friends in high school because they always had more free time than she did. After her parents had gotten divorced a couple of years ago, Lisa's mother had begun to rely on her a lot more. Every afternoon when school was over, Lisa had to get home to babysit for her younger brother and sister because her mother couldn't leave work until 5:30. Sometimes Lisa's mother would call and say she was going to be late, and Lisa would have to prepare dinner. Other girls didn't have to do all this. But in some ways Lisa liked the added chores. It made her feel more grown up. None of her friends' parents, she knew, would ever give them so much responsibility.

Children in the single-parent family are often called upon to mature quite rapidly. Not only must they shoulder an increased number of household tasks, but older children especially also share in the decision making of their families. If a single mother plans to move, for example, she may ask her teenage son to help her select a new place to live. Or if a single father is contemplating a job change, he may discuss it with his oldest daughter.

In a two-parent family these decisions are usually made by a husband and wife. They are the ones in charge, in authority, not their children. But in a single-parent family authority is often shared by a parent and child.

This may create problems. Children who are treated like adults can easily begin to believe that they should have the same privileges. Why shouldn't they be able to stay up late, or come in and go out whenever they want just as their parents do? For the parent, disciplining a child who has been treated as an equal may prove especially difficult. It's almost the same as trying to discipline a spouse. The parent may fear losing a close, valued relationship—one that she or he has come to rely on very heavily. And for a child, suddenly to have a parent act like a parent may be very upsetting. Yet if the parent doesn't impose any discipline or set any limits, the child will be the one who suffers in the long run.

Even when some time has elapsed since a divorce, children may still be reeling from the aftershock. Studies have shown that eighteen months after the divorce only a minority of children approve of their parents' decision and find the single-parent family an improvement over their previous family situation. While a majority, by this time, have been able to deal with the divorce and have resumed their lives, many children still suffer from depression. Others feel angry at their parents for separating.

Nevertheless, most children have gained increasing respect for the single parent who is running their family as they see that parent singlehandedly cope with a great variety of responsibilities. In contrast, their respect for the parent who has left the household has often declined.

This is probably due, in part, to the very nature of the relationship between a child and a visiting parent, which is difficult for everyone involved. Time is always a harsh reality in these relationships. In the two-parent family there is always tomorrow for a parent and children to finish that table they were making together, or see that exhibit of old toys at the museum before it leaves. But for the visiting parent the length of a visit limits what can be done, so some things just have to be passed by.

As a result parents may try to pack as much as they can into each visiting period, which usually occurs on weekends. They act like tour guides who try to take their children to as many events as possible. Others buy their children expensive gifts. Still others may feel at a loss over what to do with their children, and they may slowly drift away, their visits becoming less and less frequent.

When a visit ends, children often feel sad and may be unwilling to leave their parents. Some parents report feeling despair and they may also feel guilty for bringing sadness to their children. As children get older, they may resist visiting on weekends because so many other activities occur then. This creates new tensions and can hurt the visiting parent, who feels that her or his children don't want to visit anymore.

At best, the relationship between a child and a visit-

*Time is always too short for divorced parents
who visit their children only on weekends.*

ing parent may be uncomfortable for both of them. Since they are no longer in the home, parents often feel excluded, and they may bitterly resent it. Many parents are unsure of their role in the family. They may feel that their voice doesn't count anymore and may hesitate to discipline their children or offer advice. From the children's point of view, the parent is often unable to offer the kind of emotional support that they may need on an ongoing basis.

The visiting period often becomes an occasion for renewed conflict between a husband and wife. A husband, for example, may keep his children longer than the time agreed on, disrupting his wife's schedule. The next time he comes to pick them up, she may retaliate by not having them ready on time. This can result in bitter arguments, with the children frequently caught in the middle.

Yet some families seem to deal with the problems of divorce effectively and maintain a healthy, stable environment for their children. Their success is due to a variety of important factors:

- The ability of parents to set aside their own conflicts and put the needs of their children first.
- The emotional strength of the children.·
- The children's relationship with the visiting parent.
- The single parent's skill in raising children.
- The support the single parent receives from outside the family.

When Bill and Sandy were divorced three years ago, Bill found an apartment in the same part of town so he could be near their two children—Mark and Lisa. Although Sandy was given custody of the children, they spend every weekend with their father. With Bill they usually keep to a fairly regular routine, which includes fixing dinner at home and watching TV, although occasionally they go out to the movies. Sandy and Bill maintain a stiff, but polite, relationship. When Sandy has to travel in her job, which often happens, Bill takes the kids. And if an important decision has to be made regarding them—such as whether Mark should be made to repeat the third grade—Sandy and Bill make it together. This provides a relatively stable and supportive environment for Mark and Lisa.

THE NEED FOR FRIENDS

With all their responsibilities it's probably no wonder that single parents often feel overwhelmed or suffer from emotional exhaustion. Some single parents are fortunate enough to have cooperative ex-spouses, while others can rely on their children for help. But most single parents find that they must turn to friends for advice and support.

Following a separation and divorce, a single person usually discovers that old friendships no longer seem fulfilling. These friendships—many of them, at any rate—probably consisted of other couples whom the single person met while part of a couple too. Now, being around these couples may simply make one feel lonely and only reemphasize the stark reality of the divorce. The other couples may also feel awkward—uncertain about what to say or how to react. Some may even blame the single person for causing the divorce. Others may fear that divorce is contagious and they will catch the disease; or, worse yet, that the single person will snatch their spouse away.

But, more than anything else, old friends drift away because the concerns of married couples and single parents are just not the same. Single parents need to form friendships with other people like themselves—people with whom they can share experiences. Sometimes an organization such as Parents Without Partners can help. Friendships can also be developed on the job, within a neighborhood or apartment complex, through a babysitting service or day-care center.

Here's what friends can mean to a single parent:

Friends can help you when your car breaks down and you need a ride to work or you have to keep an appointment with the kids' pediatrician. Friends are people you can have over for a quick dinner when you're feeling lonely and there's no other adult around to talk to. With friends you can discuss your ex-spouse, your boss, your kids, your day-care center, or your landlord. Friends understand what you're talking about because they've been there, too.

Yet, no friendship—no matter how close—can take the place of that closeness that comes through an intimate relationship. Many single parents, especially women, seem reluctant to develop these relationships, at least in the weeks and months just after their divorce. They are frequently hesitant to trust another person for fear of being hurt once again.

Even when a single parent does decide to begin dating, eligible dates may be difficult to find. Single parents usually feel uncomfortable when friends invite them to dinner and arrange to have somebody there for them to meet. But they may be just as anxious about reentering the dating "scene" and looking for someone on their own. Many single parents suffer from the same uncertainties that probably afflicted them as teenagers when they began dating for the first time: Do I look attractive enough? Will my date like me? How will I think of something intelligent to say? Will I make a fool of myself? What will I do if I don't like my date?

It is quite natural for adults to be uneasy about dating

after being away from it for, in some cases, twenty years or more. Some single parents feel out of place, too old for the whole thing, and they are simply unprepared to go through it all again. Others feel uncomfortable with today's sexual morality, which may be very different from the one they were used to in the past; and they are unwilling to play in a dating game that is governed by the rules of this new morality.

Another concern that single parents must face is how their children will react. On the one hand, children may be pleased, especially if their parents seem happy with whomever they are dating. Generally the parents are in a better mood, which makes life far more enjoyable at home. The children may also welcome having another person around to act as a kind of substitute parent and spend time with them.

On the other hand, children are often afraid that their parents will be able to give them far less attention as they become much more involved in an intimate relationship. In fact, children who have come to depend so heavily on one parent may be afraid of being totally abandoned. They may also feel that the new person in their parent's life will totally replace the parent who has left. Most children retain a fierce loyalty to their visiting parent, who continues to hold a very special place in their lives.

All these issues become especially important if the single parent decides to remarry, as many do. This creates an entirely different family situation. The new adult who enters the family not only becomes the spouse of the single parent, but a stepparent as well. And these roles may be difficult to play. Some stepfathers who have married single women with children report feeling left out of their families. The single parent and children had gotten so used to doing things on their own that they seemed unwilling to change in order to admit the new stepparent. Other stepparents feel that they are in constant competition with the visiting parent. Their stepchildren may resent them and be unwilling to admit them into the family. Many stepchildren seem to live under the illusion that all stepparents are like the wicked stepmother of the fables. In addition, if a stepparent has children from a former marriage, this often creates an entirely new set of challenges.

Today about 80 percent of the people who divorce get married again; and the majority of these remarriages involve children. Many of these families are successfully able to handle all the new relationships that are created between parents, stepparents, and stepchildren. But it generally requires tremendous flexibility on the part of everyone. A new stepparent must be able to adapt to an unfamiliar situation. A visiting parent may have to assume a somewhat different role. And the single parent and children must be willing to open up their small family unit, enlarge it, and share its intimacy with others.

7

DEATH IN
THE FAMILY

The third chapter in the book of Ecclesiastes from The
Old Testament begins:

> There is an appointed time for everything, and a
> time for every affair under the heavens. A time to
> be born, and a time to die; a time to plant and a
> time to uproot the plant. . . . A time to weep
> and a time to laugh; a time to mourn and a time
> to dance.

Perhaps these words, better than any others, summarize
the family life cycle. Death brings an end to that life
cycle. In America today there are approximately 13 million widowed people—women and men. Many of them
are over age 65; and the vast majority of them are wom-
en, since women generally marry men older than they are
and outlive them. But some widowed people are much
younger, and they are frequently left alone with children
to support. As single parents they encounter the same
problems that we examined in the preceding chapter, as
well as some different ones. We will look at the world of
the widowed more closely a little later.

It used to be, in past eras, that death occurred within the family setting. The dying spent their last weeks at home in familiar surroundings; and when the time came for them to die, the last people they saw were other family members. Funerals were held at home where mourners came to pay their last respects, and the dead were frequently buried a short distance away in a family burial plot. Death was very much an accepted part of family living.

Today the dying spend their final days in a convalescent home or hospital, frequently surrounded by the finest medical equipment money can buy. They are far removed from a familiar family setting, far removed, in fact, from society itself.* Our society exalts youth and life; it has banished death. We prefer not to think about death and try to push it out of sight into special institutions that care for the dying. We don't even like to talk about death among ourselves, and especially not with young children. Euphemisms such as "passed away" are commonly used so that the word *death* never has to enter our vocabulary.

Yet, despite all our efforts to hide from death—or perhaps because of our inability to confront death—it is extremely frightening for most of us. And when death occurs to a beloved family member, all his or her loved ones may suffer. As one young man recalls:

> My father had gone into the hospital for what was supposed to be a routine operation. Late that

*Recently a concept called the *hospice* has given dying patients an alternative to the hospital. Instead the patients remain at home with their families who help care for them. Medically trained personnel come to the home and provide any additional care necessary to keep the patients comfortable. These patients have decided to give up any hospital treatment designed to prolong their lives. They generally die at home, or if their conditions grow extremely bad, may spend their final hours in a hospital.

afternoon, following surgery, I arrived at the hospital where I confidently expected to see Dad back in his room on his way to feeling better. Instead, as I got off the elevator, I was met by my mother and brother in a state of despair.

It seemed that Dad had suffered a massive heart attack on his way up from the recovery room and had died moments earlier, despite every effort by the hospital to save him.

My first reaction was disbelief. I just couldn't accept the fact that this had really happened. Then, even as the event sank in, I still couldn't believe that Dad wasn't going to be around anymore. We had depended on him so much. My mother had always called him her strength, and without him she seemed lost. All of us were overcome with grief. My brother and I, who had not cried for years, broke down more than once during the funeral and the days afterward. It took so long to accept the enormous change in our lives. In fact, it wasn't till at least a year later that I had really adjusted to it. My mother, I'm afraid, has never really adjusted.

COPING WITH DEATH

Experts have made a list of the twelve events in a person's life that create the most stress and require the most adjustment. As you can see, the death of a spouse is number 1.

Life Events Requiring Adjustment

Death of spouse
Divorce
Marital separation

Death of a close family member
Sex difficulties
Major personal injury
Fired from work
Jail term
Marriage
Marital reconciliation
Retirement
Death of close friend

In her book *Widow,* Lynn Caine describes the death of her husband, from cancer, and how she dealt with it. Ms. Caine writes that when Martin first learned of his fatal illness, part of him accepted the fact that he was going to die, but part of him still couldn't believe it. Scientists point out that it is quite natural for patients to react to being told that they have a terminal illness with disbelief. Most of us think we're immortal, that death will never claim us, or at least not until we're very old. If a doctor tells us we have a fatal disease and are going to die, our normal reaction is "no, not me; it's impossible."

Ms. Caine explains that in their last year together, she and her husband tried to enjoy their lives as much as possible. They had warm, tender moments together. The Caines also purchased a variety of rather expensive items that they had denied themselves. And they spent a last summer vacation in the country with their two children. During this vacation Martin's cancer grew steadily worse, and with it, his suffering. But, as the author writes, Martin tried to be heroic and not allow himself to show his emotions. If he had any fear of death, Martin never discussed it, and wouldn't allow Lynn to talk about it either. Nor did he discuss his sadness and despair over the fact that he would not be around to see his children grow up.

Psychologists have studied this feeling of loss experienced by dying patients. They lose their health, their jobs, their children, and finally everything. Many patients feel angry that others around them are going to live, while they are going to die. "Why, me?" the patient rightly asks. In the last stages of a fatal illness, many patients seem to accept their death. In Martin's case, acceptance was accompanied by withdrawal from the world around him. This is quite common. The concerns of the dying are quite different from those of the living. And they often need to be alone, to prepare themselves, as that final moment approaches.

Following Martin's death, Lynn experienced various stages of grief, which she describes in her book. At first there was a numbness or shock, even though Lynn had known for some time that her husband was going to die. This numbness, she says, helped her get through those early days of being a widow as she went through the funeral arrangements. But eventually, the numbness wore off and the pain of grieving began. Ms. Caine writes of the terrible feeling of being alone with no other adult to talk to or share her life with. Although she was working fulltime, she was extremely afraid of not being able to get along financially without Martin's income and not being able to raise her children without his help.

Ms. Caine talks about going through a period of "craziness," which occurs for many widows, when she did things that seemed completely irrational. Out of the clear blue, Lynn called up a man whom she had once known but not talked to for many years and asked for his help. She gave up her established way of life in the city and moved her family to the suburbs, hoping to save money and give her children a better environment. There she was even more lonely and depressed; and the world seemed even more frightening and overwhelming. She also described a feeling quite common to many widowed people—anger toward the person who has died, for leaving them alone to cope with life on their own.

Gradually, though, Ms. Caine began to recover. Little by little, she worked through her negative feelings and started to rebuild her life. She returned to the city and found others with similar experiences to whom she could turn for help and advice. Having a job helped, Lynn writes. "No matter how alone I was in the world, I had a place where I belonged. Work to do." She also learned how to manage the finances and run the household on her own. As a result of the entire experience, Lynn Caine became a more independent, self-reliant woman; but it was a painful process that took a long time.*

A MAN ALONE

Coping with the death of a spouse is not only a woman's problem. There are more than 2 million widowers in this country. And studies have shown that these men are more prone to dying from suicide, stroke, and heart disease than those who are married.

For a man, the death of a spouse may be somewhat different than it is for a woman. Many a woman achieves her sense of identity in large part from her role as a wife. Most men, on the other hand, seem to rely more on their jobs to give them their identities. So, when their spouses die, their identity change may not seem so great. During the grieving period men can also throw themselves into their work and find some relief.

Nevertheless, men still suffer through all the stages of grief that Lynn Caine describes in her book, and experience the same intense feelings of loneliness, despair, and anger. Often, it is harder for them to deal with these feel-

---

*Research suggests that widowhood is hardest for people who become widows early in their lives when there are not many others in a similar situation. The individual often feels out of step with other people of the same age and can find little support from peers.

ings because they have been raised in a culture that doesn't encourage men to express their feelings openly. Now, more and more widowers are turning for help to organizations such as Parents Without Partners and the American Association of Retired Persons. Here they can share their feelings with others who have suffered a similar loss.

One of the most difficult problems facing widowers—and widows too—is how to resume a social life. Many widowed people report losing the friendship of couples that they had when they were married. Somehow these couples just feel uncomfortable around a widowed person. Perhaps they don't know what to say; perhaps they don't like having death get that close because it reminds them that they or their spouse will die eventually, too. Widowed people may be no less uncomfortable because they feel as if they don't belong, like a "fifth wheel."

Reestablishing a social life may be especially difficult for widowers, according to some experts. This is partly because many men have looked to their wives to manage social arrangements and are uncomfortable taking on this role themselves. In addition, widowers may not know other men in the same situation, for they have usually died before their wives.

Most widowed people think about dating again and developing an intimate relationship with someone new, but this often poses its own set of problems. Among the elderly, the number of widows so far outnumbers the widowers that there are not enough men to go around. While this may seem like a marvelous opportunity for the men, many report feeling awkward about beginning to date again after so many years. Widowed people—both men and women—also feel guilty about dating, as if they are betraying a dead spouse. And if the widowed person happens to be a single parent, he or she must take the children's reactions into consideration, too.

Many of the elderly, of course, carry on alone. They must face the illnesses and disabilities of declining old age by themselves. Studies have shown that elderly singles are far less capable of getting along on their own than elderly couples. Older couples can manage much longer because they can weather crises together; and if one is disabled, the other can fill in and help out. Alone, an old person has no one to lean on day to day. And she or he is often forced more rapidly, by the effects of declining health, to give up an independent life style for a nursing home or hospital.

HOW CHILDREN REACT
TO A PARENT'S DEATH

Children experience intense emotional reactions to the death of a parent, and they need the help of the remaining parent to work through these emotions. But this parent may be so consumed with grief that she or he is unable to help. Children sense this and often keep their emotions inside, not wanting to upset their parent any further. As a result, parents may wrongly suppose that their children have gotten over the death, while, in reality, they are usually overcome with unspoken grief.

A child's first reaction to death is generally shock and disbelief. When talking about the event, especially with very young children, it's important for parents to explain to them what death really means. To say that the dead parent has simply gone on a long trip may leave a child with the false hope that this person will someday return. And telling children that death is like sleep may make

The pain of a parent's death
is shared by
the whole family.

them afraid to go to sleep themselves. Children need to know that death is forever, and unlike any other event in life. Often children will continue asking questions about the death long after the event has occurred. Psychologists urge parents to be honest with their answers and to discuss a child's concerns as much as possible.

In her book *Death's Single Privacy,* Joyce Phipps describes the sudden death of her husband and how she and her young children dealt with it. Ms. Phipps explains that her oldest son Keith, aged 5, kept announcing to friends that his Dad had died and waited for their reaction so that he could be sure the death was real. Her younger son, Craig, who was aged 2½, "took to crushing dandelions, repeating the word 'dead' after each act of violence." This was how he tried to understand what death really meant.

Ms. Phipps recalls that both boys experienced intense grief over their father's death, but they expressed it differently. Keith was much like his mother—he talked about the death and this helped him cope with it. Craig, on the other hand, said very little at first because the reality of death took longer for him to understand. Then, one morning four months after his father had died, he cried out: "I want my Daddy. I want my Daddy." Ms. Phipps says that Keith went to comfort his younger brother and explain that their Daddy was dead. "It's true, it's really real," Keith said; and Craig seemed to understand.

Each child reacts to a parent's death in different ways. Some feel guilty, as if they are responsible. A little boy, for example, may remember the time he said to his mother "I wish you were dead." And when she dies a few months later, he may believe that his wish had magical powers and caused her death. Or a little girl may feel that she has been bad and when her father dies, she may think that this is her punishment.

Children often become fearful that when one parent—usually the father—is gone, there may not be enough money for the family to survive. They also worry that the remaining parent may be taken from them. Joyce Phipps writes that she constantly stressed to her children that their family was still a real family even though there was only one parent, and it would continue to remain so. But this is not always enough to satisfy a child.

Craig and Keith, for instance, continued to feel the absence of a father tremendously. While still missing their own father, as time went on they began longing for a replacement, constantly asked their mother openly for one.

In her book *Widow,* mentioned earlier in this chapter, Lynn Caine describes the problems she encountered as a single parent. Sometimes it was difficult to give her children the attention they needed and still have time to handle all the problems thrust upon her by her husband's death. As she explained to her daughter, Buffy: ". . . it's hard when a little girl and her mother don't have a lot of time together, isn't it?"

Widowed people who are also single parents must handle an enormous number of responsibilities. These include not only the day-to-day tasks of running a household or holding down a full-time job. There are also the needs of children as they work through their grief and try to continue with their lives. And there are the parents' own needs as they try to cope with the loss of a spouse— a companion, an intimate, a helpmate—and start living again.

Eventually time heals most of the wounds caused by the death of a loved one, but until then, the grief often seems difficult to bear.

As the poet Edna St. Vincent Millay wrote:

Life must go on
And the dead be forgotten;
Life must go on;
Though good men die.

Anne, eat your breakfast;
Dan, take your medicine
Life must go on;
I forget just why.

8

THE FAMILY—TODAY AND TOMORROW

We began this study by looking at the American family during the colonial period and over the next three centuries. Then we examined various aspects of the family as it exists today: the family cycle, common problems in the family, divorce, the single-parent family, and, finally the impact of death. From all this information, what conclusions can we draw about the American family today? And what predictions, if any, do we dare make about the American family in the future?

Many experts believe that the family is in the midst of a grave crisis. They point to such things as the rising number of divorces annually; the many children born out of wedlock; the large number of children living with only one parent; and the vast increase in couples who are living together without marriage. Other experts just as strongly contend that the family is very much alive and healthy and thriving as never before. They focus on statistics such as the rising number of marriages annually; the renewed emphasis on formal wedding ceremonies; the high rate of divorced people who remarry; and the birth rate, which is once again beginning to inch upward.

	1970	PRESENT
married people	95 million	102.6 million
percent of total	72%	65%
marriages annually	2.2 million	2.5 million
percent of married couples with children under 18	57%	51%
married women working	18.4 million	25.5 million
percent of total	41%	52.2%
percent of married women working with children aged 6–17 years	49%	62.5%
percent of married women working with children under 6 years of age	30%	45%
divorced people	4.3 million	11 million
percent of total	3%	11%
divorces annually	708 thousand	1.2 million
children under age 18 living with one parent	8 million	12.5 million
single-parent families headed by women	2.9 million	5.6 million
couples living together	523,000	2.8 million
widowed people	11.8 million	12.8 million
percent of total	9%	13%

Whether or not you believe the family is dying or thriving, one thing is certain: Vast changes have occurred in the past, and are continuing to occur to the American family today. (Some of these changes can be seen on the chart on the opposite page, which includes only the period from 1970 to the present.)

At the present time more people are living in a greater variety of family forms than at any other period. While the vast majority of Americans over age 18 are married, just as they always have been, notice that the percent of the total has dropped since 1970. There are also far more divorced people, single-parent families, and children who are living with only one parent. Since an overwhelming number of people who divorce eventually remarry, this has led to a large increase in families with stepparents, stepchildren, and stepsiblings. In addition, the percentage of married couples with children has declined, which clearly reflects the increasing number of husbands and wives who choose to remain childless. In contrast, more single women are choosing to have children.

While about one-half million children were living with single mothers who had never married in 1970, there were about 1.8 million by the early 1980s. Finally, the number of couples living together has skyrocketed— quintupling in a little over a decade.

As a result of the variety of family forms, it seemed necessary to define the family in very broad terms. Consequently, the definition chosen at the beginning of this book was the one developed by the American Home Economics Association:

Two or more persons who share resources
. . . values and goals, and have commitments to
one another over time, regardless of blood, legalities, adoption, or marriage.

*A typical American
family in the 1980s*

A second change that has occurred in the American family is the roles that people play in it. During the colonial period a husband and wife often worked together tilling and harvesting their fields. They also shared some of the responsibility for domestic chores and childrearing. During the industrial revolution the home and the workplace became separated. Generally, a man went off to a factory or office to work, leaving his wife at home to run the household and raise his children. Throughout the twentieth century, statistics show that more and more women were entering the workplace. Then, over the past two decades, this number increased dramatically. Today the majority of married women work, and many have children who are of school age or younger. Thus, in many families a man and woman share the role of breadwinner.

Most Americans seem to accept the changes that have occurred in the American family during the present era. For example, recent polls show that 75 percent of the American public believe single people should be able to have children; a majority see nothing wrong with couples living together; most think that married women should have the opportunity to work outside the home. Yet all Americans may not be quite so accepting as they appear.

For instance, although a man may be willing to have his wife work, he often feels uncomfortable about it, especially if she makes more money than he does. As one man explained:

> It was hard for me to accept the fact that my wife earned more than I did because her profession— she's a lawyer—pays much better than mine does. I felt inadequate, like I wasn't really a man. I'd been brought up to believe that real men earned enough to support their wives. It took a long time for me to finally adjust to the situation and begin to enjoy some of the things that her paycheck could buy for us.

While men generally agree that, with their wives working, they should take on a larger share of the household chores, most men don't do so. Men also have very fixed notions about who should take care of children: women. They believe that a woman should put her family ahead of her career and stay at home once children are born. Many wives seem to agree. And this has created tremendous conflicts for women who find themselves having to choose between a family or a career, or trying to maintain both simultaneously.

Traditional attitudes regarding family roles are often very hard to break. No less difficult are our attitudes regarding the type of family structures we ought to live in. Americans say they accept the great diversity of structures. Yet, we frequently act as if the traditional nuclear family, consisting of a working father and a mother who remains at home to run the household and raise the children, is the only type of family structure that exists. We may prefer it that way, but, in fact, these families are a distinct minority.

Nevertheless, we seem to provide very little support for other family structures. For example, there is a need for more child-care facilities in this country by many single parents—men and women—as well as by married working women with children who are not yet school age. So far this need has not been adequately addressed by government leaders or private corporations, few of which provide day care for their employees' children. Some companies do allow women employees (such as computer programmers) to work at home. Two women can also share a job, with each working two or three days a week at the company, an arrangement that allows women to spend more time with their children. But most companies have also been unwilling to offer employees more flexible working hours. This might allow a single mother to leave her job early enough in the afternoon so she could get home before her child returns from school.

Flexible working hours would also prove extremely beneficial for men. Those who head single-parent families could spend more time with their children. And those in conventional nuclear families could take on a greater role in parenting. At present most men are locked into 9–5 jobs, five days a week, leaving women with the major responsibility for childrearing. Interviews with contemporary women suggest that they are often reluctant to leave children all day and take jobs, if they can financially avoid it. All the child care in the world—whether provided by private enterprise or the government—won't change this situation. Mothers are happiest when their children are being taken care of by their parents—if not their mothers, then their fathers. But for this to happen, and for women to be freed from the major responsibility of child care, men's roles must change. This means a change in their traditional work day.

While Americans have grappled with changes in family structures and roles, they've also had to come to terms with changes in the family's functions., During the colonial period families seemed almost self-sufficient. Family members produced their own food and clothes and protected themselves in the wilderness. Children were educated at home and often provided with the training they needed to support themselves in adulthood.

Over the centuries the family lost these functions and they were gradually taken over by other institutions—mainly the school and the government. Today, the major functions of the family are to rear children—feed, clothe, and socialize them—and to provide emotional support and fulfillment for all family members. Self-fulfillment, in fact, has become a primary goal for millions of Americans. They search for it not only in their family relationships, but in their jobs and recreational activities, too.

Just as many people seek a new job when the old one is no longer fulfilling, they may eventually try to leave a family that no longer provides fulfillment. This has produced a dramatic increase in the number of divorces over the last few decades.

Most people seem to expect that their family relationships will not last forever. Recent surveys indicate that a majority of Americans do not believe that a married couple will stay together throughout their lifetime. Impermanence has become a way of life.

Yet, some statistics seem to suggest that these attitudes may be changing. The divorce rate, for example, appears to be leveling off. Americans who have jumped from one relationship to another in search of self-fulfillment have often found only emptiness. The reason is that self-fulfillment frequently means selfishness, and a "me-first" attitude is rarely satisfying for anyone involved in a relationship. Real fulfillment comes not only through the opportunity to develop your own identity, but also a commitment to help others develop their identities, too. Fulfilling relationships between individuals are based on a give and take, a willingness to compromise, and a desire to achieve mutual happiness.

THE FUTURE

After this brief review of the American family today what can we now say about the future? Divorce rates may continue to level off and family units may indeed grow more stable. Nevertheless, we can still expect to see a large number of people—and perhaps an ever-increasing number—continue to live in the present variety of family forms. And some new ones may even develop that we cannot as yet foresee. But this does not indicate that the family is declining or dying, only that we are trying to define it in broader terms.

The American family remains alive and well because

of one very simple fact: No other institution can do what the family does. In a world that daily grows more and more impersonal, the family is one place where each person can feel appreciated as a unique individual. It is the one place where we can feel respected and loved just for being ourselves.

In a survey conducted only a few years ago, 96 percent of the population said that they were committed to the idea of two people sharing a life and home together. It is this commitment that makes the American family our most enduring and dynamic institution.

FOR FURTHER
READING

Bane, Mary Jo. *Here To Stay: American Families in the Twentieth Century*. New York: Basic Books, 1976.

Caine, Lynn. *Widow*. New York: Bantam Books, 1974.

Caplow, Theodore, et al. *Middletown Families*. Minneapolis: University of Minnesota Press, 1982.

Duvall, Evelyn. *Marriage and Family Development*. New York: J.B. Lippincott, 1975.

Fox, Vivian, and Quit, Martin. *Loving, Parenting and Dying: The Family Cycle in England and America, Past and Present*. New York: Psychohistory Press, 1980.

Friedan, Betty. *The Feminine Mystique*. New York: W. W. Norton, 1963.

*Greenleaf, Barbara Kaye. *Children Through the Ages: A History of Childhood*. New York: McGraw-Hill, 1978.

*Handlin, Oscar, and Handlin, Mary. *Facing Life: Youth and the Family in American History*. Boston: Little Brown, 1974.

Janeway, Elizabeth. *Between Myth and Morning: Women Awakening*. New York: William Morrow, 1974.

_____.*Cross Sections from a Decade of Change*. New York: William Morrow, 1982.

Jones, Landon Y. *Great Expectations: America and the Baby Boom Generation.* New York: Coward, McCann and Geoghegan, 1980.

Knox, David. *Exploring Marriage and the Family.* Glenville, Ill.: Scott, Foresman, 1979.

Kirkendall, Lester, and Whitehurst, Robert, eds. *The New Sexual Revolution.* New York: Donald W. Brown, 1971.

*Krementz, Jill. *How It Feels When a Parent Dies.* New York: Knopf, 1981.

Kübler-Ross, Elizabeth. *On Death and Dying.* New York: Macmillan, 1969.

Lasch, Christopher. *Haven in a Heartless World: The Family Besieged.* New York: Basic Books, 1977.

Phipps, Joyce. *Death's Single Privacy.* New York: The Seabury Press, 1974.

*Richards, Arlene, and Willis, Irene. *How to Get It Together When Your Parents Are Coming Apart.* New York: David McKay, 1976.

Singer, Laura J. *Stages: The Crises That Shape Your Marriage.* New York: Grosset and Dunlap, 1980.

Wallerstein, Judith S., and Kelly, Joan Berlin. *Surviving the Breakup: How Children and Parents Cope with Divorce.* New York: Basic Books, 1980.

Weiss, Robert S. *Marital Separation.* New York: Basic Books, 1975.

_____. *Going It Alone.* New York: Basic Books, 1979.

Yankelovich, Daniel. *New Rules.* New York: Bantam Books, 1981.

Magazines and newspapers such as *Better Homes and Gardens, Ladies Home Journal, Parents Magazine, Redbook, U.S. News and World Report, Psychology Today, New York Times,* and *Ms.* often have articles on aspects of the family and family relationships.

*Denotes books of interest to younger readers.

INDEX

Adams, John, 8
Adolescence, 11, 14, 44–46, 64, 77
Adolescence (Hall), 11
Adoption, 21
Adultery, 69; double standard, 15
Alimony payments, 74, 82
American Association for Marriage and Family Therapy, 64
American Association of Retired Persons, 101
American Home Economics Association, 21, 109
Antenuptial agreement, 30

Baby boom generation, 13, 46
Better Homes and Gardens, 35, 39
Birth control, 15, 19, 25–26, 34
Birth rates, 12, 13, 107
Browning, Robert, 49
Budgeting, 57

Caine, Lynn, 98–100, 105
Caine, Martin, 98–99
Century of the Child, 13
Childbearing, postponement of, 19, 35
Childbirth, 36, 37
Child care services, 39, 83–84, 112
Child custody, 74
Childhood, children: colonial era, 7; and divorce, 71, 75–79, 86–90; loss of parent by death, 102–105;

needs, 41–44; 19th century, 10–12; in single-parent families, 81 and *n*., 85–90, 92–93, 108, 109; 20th century, 10–12, 108
Child labor, 10; prohibited, 13
Childlessness, by choice, 34–35, 109
Child-rearing responsibility, 6–8, 9–11, 12, 13–14, 35, 37–40, 111, 112, 113; discipline, 41, 62–64; 86; parental conflicts, 41, 43–44, 62–64
Child support payments, 74, 82
Cohabitation, 27–29, 107, 108, 109
College enrollment, 11, 13; women, 19
College students, 26–27
Colonial era, 3–8, 16, 19, 24, 111
Communication, need for, 29–30, 33–34, 54–55
Cooke, Jay, 10
Custis, John, 5

Dating, 15, 24–25; single parents, 91–93; widow(er)s, 101
Day-care centers, 84, 112
Death, 20, 23, 24, 49, 50, 52, 95–106; coping with, 97–102; reaction of children to, 102–105
Death's Single Privacy (Phipps), 104
Diary of a Young Girl (Frank), 45
Divorce, 5, 12, 15, 19, 24, 67–79, 81, 90, 97; causes of, 69–71; de-

Nineteenth century, 8–12, 16, 111
Nuclear family, 20, 112; defined, 6

Old age, 49–50; widowed state, 101–102

Parenthood, 37–46; preparing for, 34–36; sharing by partners, 39–40; strains of, 40–41, 43–44, 46, 62–64. *See also* Child-rearing responsibility
Parents, role of: with grown children, 47–48; 19th century, 11–12; 20th century, 14, 39
Parents Without Partners, 91, 101
Phipps, Joyce, 104, 105
Post-partum blues, 37
Pregnancy, 35–36; teenage, 26
Premarital sex, 25
Promiscuity, 26
Property rights, women's, 16
Puritan, 3, 7; work ethic, 10

Remarriage, 67, 93, 107, 109
Retirement, 49–50
Rockefeller, John D., 10
Roles of spouses, 14, 16–19, 29, 34, 39–41, 111–112

Schools, role of, 11–12, 14, 20
Sense of self (identity), 29, 45, 83, 100; loss of, 57–58, 82
Separation, marital, 67, 70–71, 73, 75, 97; legal agreement, 74
Sexual intercourse, 15, 25, 50; problems, 58–59, 69
Sexual mores, 25–26; double standard, 15, 25; liberalized, 14–15, 20; of teenagers and students, 26–27
Shared jobs, 112
Single men, 3, 4, 100–102, 112, 113
Single-parent families, 20, 21, 44, 47, 77, 81–93, 95, 104–105, 107, 112–113; child's problems, 85–90, 92–93; money problems, 82; parent's dating, 91–92, 101; parent's problems, 81–85, 90–93; statistics, 81 and *n.*, 108, 109
Single women, 3, 81–85, 95, 99–100, 101–102, 108, 109, 112
Statistical table, 108
Stepchildren, 92–93, 109

Teenagers, 44–46; pregnancies, 26; sex, 26–27
20th century, 12–19, 24, 111
Two-income families, 38–39, 58, 111
Two- or three-generation families, 6, 21, 23, 46–48, 61–62

Unemployment, 57–58; youth, 46–47
Urbanization, 9, 11

Virginity, double standard, 15, 25
Visitation rights, 74, 87–89, 93
Vote, women's, 16

Welfare families, 83
Widow (Caine), 98, 105
Widow(er)hood, 20, 99–100 and *n.*; men, 100–102; social life, 101; statistics, 95, 108; women, 20, 95, 99–100, 101–102, 104–105
Wife/mother: role in colonial era, 6, 8, 16, 111; role in 19th century, 9, 16; role in 20th century, 16–19, 39, 40–41, 111, 112–113; working, 19, 34, 35, 38–39, 48, 68, 82–83, 108, 111
Women: as heads of families, 81–85, 108, 112; as homemakers, 9–10, 12, 16–17, 82, 111; single, 3, 81–85, 95, 99–100, 101–102, 108, 109, 112; virginity at marriage, 15; widows, 20, 95, 99–100, 101–102, 104–105; in the workplace, 12, 16–17, 48, 68, 108, 111. *See also* Wife/mother
Women's Movement, 15–17, 19, 25, 68
Women's rights, 16, 68
Women's Rights Convention of 1848, 16
Workplace: flextime, 112–113; restricted to men, 9–10, 16; separation from home, 9, 12, 16, 111; shared jobs, 112; women in, 12, 16–17, 108; working mothers, 19, 38–39, 48, 82–83, 108, 111; working wives, 19, 34, 35, 68, 108, 111

Youth culture, 14
Youth unemployment, 46–47

ECIA Chapter 2